Teaching Stories
The Arabian Nights Adventures
Scorpion Soup
Tales Told to a Melon
The Afghan Notebook
The Caravanserai Stories
Ghoul Brothers
Hourglass
Imaginist
Jinn's Treasure
Jinnlore
Mellified Man
Skeleton Island
Wellspring
When the Sun Forgot to Rise
Outrunning the Reaper
The Cap of Invisibility
On Backgammon Time
The Wondrous Seed
The Paradise Tree
Mouse House
The Hoopoe's Flight
The Old Wind
A Treasury of Tales
Daydreams of an Octopus & Other Stories

Miscellaneous
The Reason to Write
Zigzag Think
Being Myself

Nasrudin
in the
Land of Fools

Tahir Shah

NASRUDIN
IN THE
LAND OF FOOLS

TAHIR SHAH

MMXXII

Secretum Mundi Publishing Ltd
Kemp House
City Road
London
EC1V 2NX
United Kingdom
www.secretum-mundi.com
info@secretum-mundi.com

First published by Secretum Mundi Publishing Ltd, 2022

NASRUDIN IN THE LAND OF FOOLS
VERSION 12042022

© TAHIR SHAH

Tahir Shah asserts the right to be identified as the Author of the Work
in accordance with the Copyright, Designs and Patents Act 1988.
A CIP catalogue record for this title is available from the British Library.

Visit the author's website at:

www.TahirShah.com

ISBN 978-1-914960-51-2

For Jerzy,
With most sincere thanks

CONTENTS

Second-hand Rainbow

Seeing a fine rainbow arcing across the sky, Nasrudin stopped the first fool he saw.

'Want a bargain?' he asked.

'What bargain?' answered the fool.

'I've got an exceptionally lovely rainbow for sale.'

The fool blinked hard and pointed upwards.

'You mean like that one?'

'Yes,' said Nasrudin, 'that very one. You see, I own it, and as I've used it for as long as needed, I'm putting it up for sale.'

The fool blinked again.

'But you can't own rainbows,' he said.

'Of course you can.'

'Can you?'

'Yes.'

'But what's the point of owning a rainbow?'

'Are you out of your mind?! Everyone knows the value of rainbows.'

'What is it, then?'

Nasrudin considered the question for a moment, and said:

'Well, it's obvious.'

'What is?'

'The fact that owning a rainbow isn't about the rainbow itself, but about the pot of gold that's waiting at the end of it!'

The fool's eyes lit up.

'You mean there's a pot of gold at the end of that one?'

'You mean *my* one?' Nasrudin corrected.

'At the end of *your* rainbow,' the fool whispered.

'Yes indeed… You see, there happens to be the very best pot of gold I've ever seen at the end of *my* rainbow.'

'Is there?'

'Yes, of course there is!'

The fool blinked hard a third time.

'Are you telling me you didn't spend some of the gold yourself?'

Nasrudin sighed.

'All right, all right,' he hissed. 'I admit I spent a few gold dinars, but most of it's still there.'

'But, if you spent some of it, then it's not new, is it?' asked the fool.

Nasrudin felt his back warm with anger.

'All right! Technically speaking, it's not new. But, as I've said, both the rainbow and the pot of gold at the end of it are in fine shape.'

The fool was about to hand over his money when a storm cloud passed over the sun, and the rainbow vanished.

'Where's your rainbow gone?' he moaned.

Nasrudin scratched a thumbnail to his cheek awkwardly.

'Being a second-hand rainbow,' he said, 'there are a few idiosyncrasies like that. But you'll soon get used to them.'

'Idiosyncrasies like *what*?'

'Idiosyncrasies like the way it vanishes from time to time. When it does, rest assured, it'll pop up again with the pot of gold intact, so long as...'

'So long as *what*?'

'So long as you believe.'

The Demonstration

Nasrudin was found building a bridge from one end of his field to the other.

The Land of Fools was well used to oddity and eccentricity, but the bridge over a field for no reason at all stirred a great deal of interest.

Word spread fast, and fools started arriving from all corners of the kingdom.

By the time the bridge was complete, more than a thousand fools had gathered.

There were so many of them that they covered every inch of the field.

After having come so far, one of the fools demanded to know why Nasrudin had built a bridge for no reason at all.

The wise fool said he would explain the reason for the bridge through a demonstration.

Climbing the steps, he crossed the length of the bridge, pacing calmly over the heads of the throng, and down the other side.

Then, in silence, he slipped away so as to be left alone.

Forward Thinking

There were so many cars in the Land of Fools that finding a parking space was near impossible. At popular haunts, such as outside the teahouse, a good parking space was as rare as rare can be.

Nasrudin was so sick of trying to find a parking space that he thought long and hard about what to do.

Having tossed and turned in bed all night, he had a brainwave.

Next morning, he sold his car to the first fool who was passing his house.

Then, taking the fistful of money, he hurried to the teahouse on foot.

Once there, he bought one of the cars parked in prime position outside.

Not once did he ever move the vehicle for fear of losing the coveted parking space.

All day long he would recline on the sofa in the teahouse, as fools would congratulate him on his vehicle and, more importantly, on its prime parking spot.

Whenever he was asked for the train of thought that had led him to devise the genius of the eternally parked car, the wise fool would smirk, gloat, and declare:

'Nothing more than a case of forward thinking!'

Crooked Retaliation

Such was the stupidity of the general population in the Land of Fools that there was an inordinate amount of counterfeit currency in circulation.

Things got so bad that the king ordered for all fake, forged, or imperfect banknotes to be destroyed at once.

The previous month, Nasrudin had been paid for work with a badly torn thousand-dinar bill. Only discovering the defect when it was too late, he had attempted unsuccessfully to pass it on.

The fact the bill was of such a high denomination, and at the same time so worthless, caused him a great deal of stress.

The day before the deadline by which all damaged and counterfeit bills were to be removed from circulation, the wise fool was in a terrible state. The thousand-dinar note was burning a hole in his pocket, and all he could think about was spending it.

All, that is, except for rage at the sharp practices of his employer who had slipped him the banknote in the first place.

Nasrudin was leaving the teahouse, where he had attempted yet again to pass off the bill as bona fide currency, when he spotted a beggar in the long shadows of late afternoon.

Despite his wretched circumstances, the figure seemed familiar.

Approaching, Nasrudin realized it was none other than his former employer.

At glimpsing the silhouette of a potential well-wisher, the beggar called out:

'Have you nothing for a respectable old man who has fallen on hard times, sir?'

The wise fool grinned the grin of ultimate retaliation.

'I am feeling especially generous,' he cried. 'Others may give worthless coins, but let it be known that Nasrudin's generosity extends to a thousand-dinar note!'

Swapped Circumstances

One summer afternoon, the wise fool was relaxing in the teahouse when he overheard a stranger talking about him, or so he thought. Having listened in for a moment or two, he realized that the visitor to the Land of Fools was apparently called Nasrudin, too.

Fascinated that anyone else would share what was such an uncommon name, the wise fool stood up and introduced himself. The stranger was equally intrigued, especially because the other Nasrudin looked so much like him.

It wasn't long before the two Nasrudins were engaged in conversation.

As he sipped his tea, the Nasrudin who lived in the Land of Fools noticed that his namesake was far richer than he. His clothes were of finer quality, and he spoke of all manner of expensive possessions.

All of a sudden, the first Nasrudin had an idea, to which he gave voice:

'What if we were to swap identities?' he asked.

'What do you mean?' asked the second Nasrudin.

'Well, I would be you, and you would be me. And, since we're both Nasrudin, we wouldn't even have to change our names.'

'But wouldn't people wonder what's going on?'

'What if they do?'

The second Nasrudin frowned. But, then, the furrows of his brow melted, and he smiled.

'It sounds like fun!' he exclaimed.

So it was that, before leaving the teahouse, the two Nasrudins exchanged clothes. And, having got into each other's cars, they drove home to each other's lives.

A week slipped by... and then a month.

The first Nasrudin enjoyed the upgraded lifestyle that material wealth provided. He ate far finer foods than he was used to, and slept in the most exquisite bed.

The second Nasrudin, the one who was visiting the Land of Fools, was initially shocked at the impoverished state of his namesake. But, as the days progressed, he found himself charmed by the simplicity of the different circumstances.

Thirty days after the two Nasrudins had swapped, each had become so used to their new lives that neither gave any thought to what might have initially been regarded as a rather drastic change.

Exactly a year to the day of the swap, the two Nasrudins bumped into each other in the teahouse once again.

'How are you liking my life?' the first Nasrudin asked the second.

'Well, to tell you the truth, it took a little getting used to,' he explained. 'Your standard of living is very much lower than mine, as you have no doubt grasped for yourself. Your house is terribly draughty, with leaks all over the roof. Your bed is shockingly uncomfortable, and there's a terrible pong of sewage all night long. As for your wardrobe… well, the less said about your clothing, the better.'

The first Nasrudin thought of the draughts and the leaks, the discomfort and the stench, and the threadbare clothes, and let out the heaviest sigh.

'Give it back to me at once!' he bawled.

'Give *what* back?' asked the second Nasrudin.

'My beloved life!'

Faulty Conclusions

ay after day, Nasrudin patronized a third-rate bakery at the edge of town. The bread was very low quality, but it was so cheap that the wise fool put up with it, as he was saving so much money.

One day, when he cut a slice, he was thrilled to find a gold ring baked into the middle of the loaf bought from the bakery that very morning.

Anyone else who had made such a find would have either returned the ring, assuming it had slipped off the baker's finger while he was kneading the dough, or would have rushed to the gold bazaar to sell the unexpected boon.

Nasrudin did neither.

Instead, he jumped to the faulty conclusion that there was a gold ring baked into every loaf.

Taking a huge loan from a moneylender at a crippling rate, he hurried to the bakery and offered to buy the enterprise at a price vastly above the true value of the business.

By evening, Nasrudin was the proud owner of the bakery. He was so jubilant that he invited his best friends to the teahouse to celebrate. Even though all of them were champion fools, they were sceptical.

'Everyone knows that that's the very worst bakery in town!' said the first.

'People only go there because it's cheap,' quipped a second.

'You'll be bankrupt by the end of the week,' voiced a third.

Sitting across from them, Nasrudin gloated.

'You are all very wrong,' he said. 'You see, the loaves of bread in my new bakery are special. Each one has a solid gold ring baked into it.'

The three fools looked at one another in consternation, then at Nasrudin.

'No one will want your bread,' the first fool friend exclaimed.

'And the moneylender will be pounding at the door,' intoned the second.

'If that were to happen,' answered Nasrudin, 'I would simply bake a few loaves of my special gold-ring bread, and send him on his way!'

Uphill Challenge

hen the first snows of winter fell in the Land of Fools, Nasrudin was the first out on the slopes.

But rather than skiing down the mountain like everyone else, he was seen skiing uphill.

As all the other skiers zoomed fast down the mountain, the wise fool could only manage a few feet at a time.

Yet, despite the terrible difficulty, he seemed to be in fine spirits.

Another regular from the teahouse skied over and asked why Nasrudin was skiing uphill.

The wise fool looked at him hard, and spat:

'Any fool can ski downhill. The real challenge is to go in the other direction!'

Rooster and Egg

hile walking back from town one day, Nasrudin spotted a rooster strutting about, apparently without an owner.

Assuming the bird was a divine gift, he took it home.

Being short-sighted, he hadn't appreciated that the rooster was actually not a rooster at all, but a hen with unusually elaborate plumage.

Nasrudin regarded the supposed rooster as a sign of good things to come. Accordingly, he had a special pen made for it, and threw in handfuls of expensive grain.

One day, while the wise fool was out in town, the hen laid an egg. Following the excitement of the action, she flapped so hard she flew over the low fence.

Once again, the chicken was free.

Arriving home from the market with a basket full of vegetables for his feathered friend, Nasrudin discovered it gone.

But, to his amazement, he found the newly laid egg sitting in the corner of the pen.

Instantly, he jumped to an improbable conclusion – that the rooster was somehow living its life in reverse.

Rather than ageing as other roosters did, he assumed his bird had been born in the mature state, and had a backwards existence, from pot to egg, rather than from egg to pot.

Now that the creature was in its final form, he mused it was ready to leave the mortal world. So, taking the egg to his kitchen, he cracked it into a pan, and ate it for supper.

Cloak of Incrimination

hile staying as a guest in a friend's house on the far side of the Land of Fools, Nasrudin inadvertently left a bath running and flooded the house.

Embarrassed that he had caused such damage, he climbed out the window and down the drainpipe. Then, pretending that he had just arrived from the market, he came back in through the front door.

He found his friend bailing buckets of water from the house.

'What's happened here?' he asked, feigning shock.

'There's been a leak,' the friend answered. 'Can't imagine how it happened.'

Nasrudin was going to shoot back a glib reply when he realized that he had left his cloak in the bathroom. If he wasn't careful, it would be spotted, and would incriminate him.

So, thinking fast, he called out to his friend to close his eyes.

'Why?' the man growled. 'I'm in no mood for games!'

'Can't explain. But trust me!'

A bucket and mop in hand, the friend closed his eyes.

Nasrudin hurried back out the house. Having scurried up the drainpipe, he climbed in through the bathroom window, grabbed his cloak, and hastened out the window again.

A minute later, he was standing at the front door, dressed in his cloak.

'You can open your eyes now!' he exclaimed, beaming.

'What's going on?' his friend barked.

'I was just plugging the leak,' said Nasrudin.

Hide-and-find

As a child, none of the other kids wanted to play with Nasrudin, but it didn't bother him. He learned to play games by himself.

His very favourite way to spend the afternoon was playing hide-and-seek…

…alone.

At first, it would take him hours to find himself.

But, as time passed, he knew all the obvious places in which to search.

The time eventually came when the game would be up within a minute or two.

Sick of it, he strode over to the mirror and glowered at his reflection.

'All right! All right!' he yelled at himself. 'I'm not playing with you any longer. You're just too good!'

Occasional Leprosy

 asrudin's neighbour was widely regarded as the most repulsive man living in the Land of Fools. His house was collapsing through neglect. All around it there was litter, rusted old cars, and the stench of raw sewage.

The wise fool did his best to keep well clear of the neighbour. But, to his horror, the man would drop by day and night, as his own home was so unpleasant.

Although polite by nature, Nasrudin reached the point at which he couldn't take it any longer. He considered telling the truth, and asking yet again for the neighbour to mend his ways. But, giving the predicament much thought, he concluded that the man was far too old to change. The only course of action was to avoid him.

It was easier said than done, of course, because as a neighbour, he lived next door.

Nasrudin had an idea.

He would spread word that he had an incurable and infectious case of leprosy – a form so new and untreated that it had no overt symptoms at all.

As soon as the neighbour heard of the condition, he called to Nasrudin.

'I won't be coming to see you, my old friend. I do hope you understand!'

The wise fool feigned sorrow. But, as soon as the window was shut, he punched the air and danced around with delight.

A short time after, however, there was a long thump at the door.

A medical team was standing in the front garden, demanding to know about the case of leprosy.

Nasrudin smiled demurely.

'As has been advertised, it has no overt symptoms,' he explained.

'Is there anything else you can tell us about the condition you have?' asked the lead investigator.

'Yes,' said Nasrudin. 'You see, it's only discernible when I am in close proximity to my neighbour.'

Wasting Time in Wasting Time

n his travels, Nasrudin had once met a dervish in a distant kingdom.

While walking through the capital of the Land of Fools one afternoon, he spotted the very same holy man. From the look of it, the man was doing very well for himself. He was no longer dressed in rags, but rather was attired in a cloak fit for a king.

The two of them went to the teahouse.

Over refreshments, the former dervish explained how the change in fortune had occurred.

'As you'll no doubt remember,' he said, 'I used to be impoverished. But then, one day, I met a man whom I had once encountered in a distant realm. He explained to me how to make a fortune for myself.'

The wise fool smiled.

'I'm sure you have struggled to acquire the wealth you now enjoy.'

'On the contrary,' the traveller replied, 'it was as easy as easy can be.'

'Oh, what I would do for an easy income!' he exclaimed.

The former dervish sipped his tea.

'Well,' he said, leaning back into the sofa, 'perhaps I can help.'

'How?'

'I am merely travelling through the Land of Fools, and have no plans to use my method here. So, I suppose, I can pass it on for you to use as you need.'

Nasrudin bristled with delight.

'*Really*?!' he gasped.

The wealthy associate nodded.

'All you have to do,' he explained, 'is to set yourself up as a guru. With the right stage management, you will soon have a flock of devotees. Before you know it, you'll be as rich – if not richer – than me. After all, you're living in the Land of Fools!'

The next day, Nasrudin set up an ashram exactly as he had been instructed to do. Once he had built an auditorium and dormitory, he wrote a sacred book of gobbledygook.

Then, and only then, did he position a grand noticeboard in front of the door.

Before he knew it, there was a snaking line of fools, each one in urgent need of a guru to tell them how to live their lives.

But despite the number of fools ready and waiting for his service, Nasrudin refused to open the door.

Instead, he pinned a small note to the noticeboard.

It read: GO AWAY UNTIL YOU ARE WISE ENOUGH TO LEARN.

Being fools, the would-be pupils shied away.

A day or two later, the former dervish accosted Nasrudin in the teahouse.

'How's it going?' he asked.

The wise fool looked glum.

'It's a disaster,' he moaned. 'You see, I've told them to only come in for my wisdom once they are wise enough to learn.'

The dervish-turned-guru balked.

'Are you out of your mind?!' he yelled.

'Not in the least,' the wise fool riposted. 'After all, why should I waste my time in wasting their time?'

Transmuted States

ne winter evening, Nasrudin bought a carton of milk from a Foolslander in the bazaar.

Once home, he placed it on the window ledge and went to bed.

Next morning, the wise fool opened the window and found the milk had frozen solid.

Angry at having been duped, he took the frozen liquid back to the shop, and immediately attacked the Foolslander who had sold him the liquid the day before.

'Your product is possessed by some inexplicable alchemy!' spat Nasrudin. 'I bought a liquid, and now it's quite clearly a solid!'

'That's nothing to do with the milk I sold you!' hissed the shopkeeper.

'Of course it is!'

'No, it's not!'

Soon, the quarrel had drawn a crowd – a great many fools jeering as fools like to do.

A police officer soon arrived and demanded to be informed what was going on.

Nasrudin did his best to explain:

'This man sold me liquid, which then turned by mysterious alchemy into a solid!'

The officer demanded to be shown the offending product.

By this time, the frozen milk had melted, and was liquid once again.

Nasrudin crowed that the return was proof of the shopkeeper's devilry on a terrifying scale.

'His bewitched product is even more sordid than I had first feared!' he roared. 'Not content with transmuting from liquid into solid in the dead of night, it's now transmuted back into a liquid again!'

The crowd of fools jeered all the more.

The shopkeeper was arrested for disturbing the peace.

As for Nasrudin, he went home... the carton of cool milk in his hand.

Self-painting Paint

U nable to get a well-paid job, Nasrudin resorted to manual labour as an itinerant painter. As he had no tools or experience, no one gave him any work… no one except for a blind man who lived in an enormous mansion.

Even though the employer appeared shrewd, the wise fool assumed he could use the man's disability against him. He promised to get on with the job at double speed.

Mistrustful by nature, the blind owner of the mansion went upstairs to rest.

At the end of the afternoon, Nasrudin asked for his money.

The blind man winced.

'Have you finished the job?'

'Oh yes,' Nasrudin answered, 'done it all. You see, I work at ten times the speed of all other painters.'

'How could that be possible?'

'Simple,' the wise fool grinned. 'You see, I use special self-painting paint.'

In actual fact, Nasrudin hadn't painted a single wall, and hadn't bought any paint.

Despite living in the Land of Fools, the blind man knew when he was being hoodwinked. So, opening his wallet, he pretended to take out a handful of money, then pretended to pay it to the wise fool.

'I think you've made a mistake,' said Nasrudin. 'You see, you haven't given me any money at all.'

'Yes, I have,' riposted the blind man. 'Everyone knows that special invisible money is used to pay for self-painting paint.'

No Ordinary Air

oolslanders may have been terribly dim-witted, but they boasted and bragged like no one else.

Although not given to conceit by nature, Nasrudin couldn't help but be reeled in to their petty posturing. He would watch them in the teahouse trying to show off with shopping bags from expensive emporiums.

Even though the wise fool had no extra funds to blow on high-end goods, he did his level best to keep up.

While wandering through the bazaar, he found a stall selling all manner of used goods – the kind of thing well-heeled Foolslanders might have laughed at. He was about to traipse home when something caught his eye amid all the bric-à-brac...

A battered old green shopping bag, with the label *Harrods* emblazoned in gold across the front. Cursing himself for stooping to such low methods, Nasrudin bought it.

Next day, he arrived at the teahouse with the empty shopping bag. It wasn't long before a throng of Foolslander snobs had clustered around.

'What have you got there?' they asked.

'Just a little something I snapped up on my way to work this morning,' said Nasrudin.

'Show us what it is!' barked one of the more boisterous men.

'It's really nothing,' answered the wise fool.

'C'mon,' taunted another, 'let us have a look!'

With no other choice, Nasrudin opened his shopping bag.

'It's empty!' cried the first snob.

'No, it's not!'

'Yes, it is! All there is in there is air!'

Nasrudin glowered at the Foolslander snobs.

'That may be true,' he bawled, 'but it's air from *Harrods*!'

Cap of Desperation

In a bid to coax a little spending money from a fellow fool, Nasrudin bought a cheap woollen cap in the market and made an elaborate sign, which read:

AMAZING CAP

OF

INVISIBILITY

ONLY 10 DINARS

Two minutes after Nasrudin had placed the sign beside the cap on the street, a fool strode up and bought it.

He put it on his head excitedly.

But, no surprise, he didn't disappear.

'This cap of invisibility doesn't work right!' he exclaimed. 'I want my money back!'

Calm as a cucumber, the wise fool pointed a thumb at a smudged line of writing at the bottom of his sign.

'I can't read that!' yelled the fool.

Nasrudin cleared his throat.

'It says, "All goods bought at the buyer's risk".'

'Give me my money back!' the fool barked again. 'Or I'll call the police!'

Nasrudin refused.

Soon after, he found himself at the police station.

After a great deal of rage on the part of the cap's owner, the chief of police called on the pair to explain themselves.

'This man sold me a faulty cap of invisibility!' growled the customer.

'It does work,' Nasrudin countered.

'Well, if it's working, why doesn't it make me invisible when I put it on?!'

Nasrudin sighed.

'That's because there's a delay. As everyone knows, caps of invisibility need a few seconds to warm up.'

'How many seconds?' asked the chief of police.

The wise fool glanced around the room, then out the window.

'Depends on the conditions,' he said. 'But, in these conditions, with us being in a police station, and there being a forest outside, I'd say about fifteen seconds would be needed for the cap of invisibility to work.'

'Prove it or I'll arrest you!' roared the chief of police.

Nasrudin put the woollen cap on his head.

Fifteen seconds passed, and the customer protested.

'See!' he cried. 'Told you it doesn't work!'

'Hold on,' snapped Nasrudin. 'Everyone knows that caps of invisibility need darkness to be effective.'

'Do they?' asked the chief of police.

The wise fool nodded.

'But we can't wait until night.'

'I have an idea,' said Nasrudin. 'If we all close our eyes, it'll be as dark as night.'

Accordingly, the customer and the chief of police closed their eyes, and counted fifteen seconds.

When they opened their eyes, Nasrudin and the cap of invisibility were gone.

'Well, well, well,' mused the officer, 'looks as though the magical cap wasn't at fault after all.'

Finite Sympathy

The ramshackle home of Nasrudin's neighbour caught fire and was burnt to the ground. Even though the man was disliked by one and all, dozens of Foolslanders gathered around to offer sympathy.

Next door, Nasrudin found himself gripped by terrible jealousy – jealousy at never being given so much attention.

So, without giving it much thought, the wise fool poured petrol all over his wooden house and set it alight. To his horror, no one rushed to help extinguish the fire, or give any sympathy at all.

Blackened by smoke and ragged from the flames, he ambled to the teahouse.

'Heard your house burnt down,' gasped one of the regulars.

'Yes,' the wise fool whispered, reeling from shock.

'Too bad,' the regular answered.

'Wait a minute!' spat Nasrudin. 'When my wretched neighbour's house went up in flames, everyone gathered around and lavished attention on him.'

'That's right,' said the regular.

'Well, can you please tell me why no one's giving *me* any attention?!'

'Simple,' said the other man. 'You see, there's only a certain amount of sympathy to go round, and it's all been used up.'

King of Selfishness

Every year, the Land of Fools ground to a halt as a prize was given for the King of Selfishness.

No one could quite remember how or when the tradition had started. Such details hardly mattered. The only thing of importance was that the King of Selfishness was honoured and crowned.

All year long, entries were logged, and a shortlist was prepared.

In the mountains, a farmer was lauded for selfishly eating all the food, so that his wife and family starved.

In the forest, a little old woman was extolled for being so selfish she poisoned the stream so that no one else could drink from it.

In the city, Nasrudin was championed for too many A-grade acts of selfishness to record.

With the Land of Fools at a standstill, a gala dinner was held to determine the ultimate winner. First, the crème de la crème of Foolslanders were treated to song and dance routines, with the extravaganza being broadcast on TV far and wide.

When the audience was unable to contain their enthusiasm any longer, the shortlist was read out.

Then, after a drum roll and much hysteria, the compère opened the golden envelope.

'I have the great pleasure to announce that this year's King of Selfishness is none other than... Nasrudin!'

The hall erupted into a wild chorus of cheers, and a spotlight picked the wise fool out. He was sitting in the middle of the stalls. But, despite calls for him to come up to the stage and collect his trophy, he didn't budge.

The compère called down and invited the honoured winner to come and collect his trophy.

Nasrudin shook his head.

'What's the matter?!' someone called out.

'I'm not getting up!' hissed Nasrudin.

'Why ever not?!'

'Because I've got the best seat in the house. If I get up for a moment, someone else is sure to take it!'

Clothes With Experience

asrudin had never been a sharp dresser, but as the years passed, he grew more and more dishevelled.

One day, while in the market, he overheard a stranger point him out to another, describing him as a scarecrow. His pride dented, the wise fool went straight to a high-end clothes shop, the kind of establishment patronized by well-heeled Foolslanders.

After inspecting the stock, he selected one of the most expensive suits on sale and took it into the fitting room. Having undressed, he hung his own filthy clothes on a hanger and put on the exquisite new outfit.

Then, calmly, he hung his clothes on the rack from which he had chosen the new suit.

A moment later, he was walking towards the door of the shop.

As Nasrudin stepped over the threshold, back onto the street, he felt the hand of a security guard dragging him back inside.

'You haven't paid for the suit, sir!' he growled.

The wise fool regarded the guard with a piqued expression. As he did so, a manager swept forwards.

In his hand was the shabbiest outfit imaginable.

'These clothes of yours are well beyond worthless, sir,' he bawled. 'And that outfit you have dressed in is one of our most valuable.'

Nasrudin rolled his eyes.

'Perhaps that is your opinion,' he retorted.

'Of course it is, because it is true!' the shop manager shot back.

'Well, it's certainly not *my* opinion,' the wise fool countered.

'How ever not?'

Nasrudin jabbed a thumb to his shabby old costume.

'Those clothes have travelled with me on all manner of adventures,' he said. 'They've been up mountains and across deserts, and through me have embraced paupers and kings.'

'So?'

'So, the point I am making,' the wise fool growled, 'is that *my* clothes have experience, whereas these new clothes I have acquired from your emporium are raw and inexperienced. If anything, you should be paying me for downgrading as I have done. It'll take me years to give this new suit the experience it deserves.'

With that, Nasrudin strolled out from the shop, leaving his filthy old outfit behind.

An Unusual Condition

In a bid to be served first at the Land of Fools Airport, Nasrudin climbed into an unused wheelchair and pretended he was unable to walk. It wasn't long before a porter hurried forwards and offered to push him to the gate for boarding.

All went well at first.

Then the corner of Nasrudin's cloak got caught up in the wheel. Dutifully, the porter worked on freeing the wheel so he could push the injured man to the plane.

No amount of jostling could get the cloth free.

So much time had been lost that the wise fool was in danger of missing his flight.

Grunting awkwardly with disapproval, he leapt up from the wheelchair, jerked the corner of his cloak free, and sat down again.

The porter waved a fist in Nasrudin's direction.

'You're not disabled at all, are you?!'

'Yes, I am.'

'How dare you use a wheelchair that's reserved for people who really need it?'

The wise fool regarded the porter with a poisonous glance.

'And how dare *you* imagine that you know the intimate details of my condition?' quipped Nasrudin.

Fantasy Who's Who

In an especially turbulent nightmare, Nasrudin dreamt that he was being attacked by none other than his neighbour.

Waking in a cold sweat, he put on a bathrobe and hurried from his house.

A moment later, he was rapping hard on the neighbour's door.

Expecting to be told of an emergency, the neighbour answered.

'What is it, friend?' he said urgently, as he wiped the sleep from his eyes.

'You attacked me for no good reason!' Nasrudin cried. 'I demand you explain yourself!'

Having lived next to the wise fool for years, the neighbour knew his peculiarities well.

'You've just had another of your nightmares,' he explained calmly. 'And, as usual, I was merely a character who featured in your dream… a character you decided was depraved.'

His face flushed with rage, Nasrudin poked a finger at his neighbour's chest.

'Who are you to tell me who's who in my own fantasy?!' he yelled.

Causing a Stink

Through lying, deception, and outright fraud, Nasrudin got himself a job as a master perfumier at a leading couture house in the Land of Fools.

Having pretended he had a distinguished track record in the development of perfumes, he was given free hand in creating the new scent of the season.

With no experience in making fragrances, Nasrudin simply mixed all the available essences together.

The result was a stench equal to a thousand sewers.

Rather than being downcast, the wise fool was absolutely delighted. He rushed to the director's office, and sprayed the offending perfume everywhere.

Uproar ensued, before Nasrudin was ordered to explain himself.

'It may smell like sewers to you and me,' he said wistfully, 'but it's going to make a fortune!'

'How can you make such a preposterous claim?!' roared the well-groomed director.

'Well,' Nasrudin answered, 'when all the fools out there shun it, we'll be able to buy up all the stocks ourselves for next to nothing. Before we know it, we will have cornered the market! Then, when we own it all, we'll be able to sell it for twice the price!'

Ingenuity

During a pleasure cruise off the coast, the ship Nasrudin was travelling in hit a storm.

The vessel struck rocks, and the order was given to lower a pair of third-rate lifeboats.

Women and children were given priority.

Selfish to the core, the wise fool dressed as a woman, but his disguise was soon discovered. So, thinking fast, he reinvented himself as a little girl.

Yet again, he was sent to the back of the line.

A minute later, he had dressed up as a barrel. Then, after that, as a life vest.

Each time he appeared at the front of the queue, he was unmasked, reprimanded, and sent to the back.

Finally, he pushed to the front without any disguise at all.

'You're not a woman or a child!' the purser roared.

'That may be so,' Nasrudin riposted, 'but I have proved my boundless ingenuity.'

'So what?!'

'Well, just imagine how useful such inventiveness could be in saving lives aboard a lifeboat as flimsy as that!'

Ill-suited Ability

aving watched a nature film on television, Nasrudin had learned that llamas were a relative of the camel – a creature that was common where he lived.

However hard he tried, he was unable to get the long-necked Latin American creatures out of his head. Going against all the sensible advice he received, he spent all his savings on buying a llama and having it transported to the Land of Fools.

After months of waiting, a crate was delivered to Nasrudin's home, with one very angry llama inside. From the moment it was released, the animal attacked – spitting its cud, kicking with its hooves, and butting with its head.

First, it attacked Nasrudin.

Then it attacked the local policeman.

And, when being led towards the desert, it attacked a group of tribesmen.

A crowd gathered.

Screaming insults at Nasrudin, the throng demanded to know what was going through his head.

'My llama may seem unusual to you,' he explained, 'because you have not seen one before. But, with time, you will learn to appreciate that it's perfectly suited to the desert. Indeed, with time, and a little adaptation, it will certainly be as suited as the camels which are so plentiful in these parts.'

One of the fools raised a hand.

'If camels are perfectly suited to the desert,' he said, 'and they're so plentiful, then why do we have a need for llamas at all?'

Nasrudin regarded the question with contempt.

'Might I remind you that this is the Land of Fools?!' he growled.

'*So*?'

'So, spouting such wisdom, as you are doing, you appear to be in a country ill-suited to your ability.'

Lens of Imagination

While hiking in the desert, Nasrudin spotted a footprint in the sand.

Not an ordinary indentation, there was something lovely about it, as though it had been made by the most beautiful foot that ever touched the surface of the earth. Before he knew it, the wise fool had imagined the form of a radiant woman, who he assumed walked on such a foot.

With great care, he scooped up the footprint and put it in the plastic bag that had held his lunch. His heart pounding, he set off to search for the owner of the footprint.

For days, weeks, and months, Nasrudin crisscrossed the Land of Fools, asking anyone and everyone if they could recognize the footprint.

Naturally, having not kept its form, the footprint was no more than a handful of sand.

After many months of disappointment, Nasrudin stopped at one last teahouse in a distant corner of the kingdom.

Dejectedly, he pulled out the crumpled plastic bag and showed off the sand, which he claimed to be the footprint of his true love.

'Can't see any footprint,' said one of the fools. 'All I can see is sand.'

Nasrudin blinked hard.

'That's because its form has changed.'

'Changed into what?'

'Changed into a lens.'

'A lens?'

'Yes.'

'What kind of lens?' asked the fool.

'A lens of imagination,' answered Nasrudin.

Life Lessons

In a moment of unusual imprudence, Nasrudin blew his savings on a heap of worn-out rubber tyres. Two minutes after making the rash purchase, a passing idiot asked what he was going to do with such rubbish.

It was then that the wise fool was hit by inspiration.

'I'm starting a tyre circus,' he said.

Word of the unusual entertainment spread like wildfire through the Land of Fools.

For a good long while, Nasrudin dined out on all the attention he was receiving. Whenever anyone asked when the tyre circus would start performing, he would simply explain that training was going well.

Each week, expectation mounted.

Then, one day, the wise fool had an idea. He would start selling tickets for the circus. Although he didn't have any actual routines, he was sure that he would work something out.

After all, the locals in the Land of Fools had appallingly low standards.

But, having taken hard-earned money from everyone in the teahouse, the point came at which Nasrudin had no choice but to put on a show.

In the back garden of his home, he built a stage – complete with satin curtains, footlights, and all kinds of circus equipment.

The evening of the performance arrived.

A single drum rolled, the curtains parted, and a spotlight picked out a pile of ramshackle old tyres in the middle of the stage.

With the audience craning forwards in their seats, Nasrudin stepped out from the wings.

'Picture, if you will, a land far in the distance,' he intoned, his voice loaded with emotion. 'A land in which a terrible monster has turned the humble people into rubber tyres. A shocking place; what occurred here is a cautionary tale for us all.'

Silence prevailed – silence inspired by confusion.

A Foolslander stood up at the back.

'How can this ever be a lesson for any of us?' he called out gruffly, speaking for the rest of the audience.

Nasrudin sighed.

'Alas, the list of life lessons one can draw from such sordid events is too great to mention in full.'

'Please tell us one lesson!' implored a woman at the front.

Nasrudin gazed at the tyres, and let out a shriek of angst and pain.

'The greatest lesson we can learn from this scene is to think twice before blowing a fortune on a heap of old rubber tyres!' he wailed.

Desert Igloo

While trying to get through the intolerable heat of the summer afternoon, Nasrudin took to fanning himself with a newspaper and trying to imagine he was in an Arctic landscape.

His brow streaming with perspiration, he rubbed both thumbs in his eyes.

Then, as he strained to focus, his gaze caught a small advertisement on the back page of the newspaper.

It read:

LUXURY PREFABRICATED
IGLOOS FROM GREENLAND
AT DISCOUNT PRICES!

Cooled at the mere thought of the idea, the wise fool ordered one of the igloos at once. But, being stingy by nature, he opted for the least expensive transport.

A month later, a sea container was delivered to his home.

Nasrudin, who was beside himself with glee, signed the paperwork, unlocked the doors, and was thrown backwards by a wave of water.

Enraged, he telephoned the igloo broker and demanded his money back. The salesman on the other end refused, and suggested that the customer simply refreeze the water back into blocks of ice.

'Even if I were to follow your suggestion...' the wise fool yelled, 'how on earth would I know how they all fitted together?!'

The salesman cleared his throat.

'I'm quite willing to send you instructions,' he said.

A little time passed, in which Nasrudin got even hotter under the collar.

The more heated he became, the more he yearned for vengeance.

Then, one especially scorching afternoon, he had an idea.

Digging out the phone number of the igloo salesman, he dialled it.

Once pleasantries were over, the wise fool said:

'As you will remember, I purchased a top-of-the-range igloo from you, and had it shipped to me here in the Land of Fools.'

The salesman held back his laughter. After all, as Greenland's foremost conman, he had simply filled the container with water and shipped it out.

'Yes, sir, of course, I remember. How thrilled I am to hear of another satisfied customer. Congratulations on refreezing the blocks of ice and fitting them together.'

Nasrudin gave a rancorous grunt.

'Simple once I got the hang of it,' he replied. 'Even though igloos are for a different climate, our great luxurious sand palaces are very much the same.'

The salesman's interest piqued, he asked whether such a palace had ever been transported overseas.

'Oh yes,' Nasrudin answered. 'As it so happens, I'm in the sand palace transportation business, and could give you one at a discount.'

By the end of the conversation, the conman had placed an order, paying for a sand palace by credit card.

A month later, a sea container arrived in Nuuk, the capital of Greenland.

Eager to impress everyone else in the small community, the salesman had it delivered to the plot of land he had bought in the middle of the town.

Once the container had been hauled to the right spot, the doors were opened.

Rather than finding a palace inside, the salesman found nothing but sand, floor to ceiling, and wall to wall.

Overcome with rage, he called the wise fool, who was lying on his back, fanning himself with a newspaper.

The crooked salesman vented his rage.

When he had done so, Nasrudin feigned surprise.

'I am so sorry to hear of your distress,' he said. 'If it would be helpful, I could send over a set of sand palace plans.'

Makak!

ne evening, Nasrudin was reclining in the teahouse when he overheard two visitors to the Land of Fools talking about a curious grant, given by the United Nations.

As he understood it, the UN had a special department for the preservation for endangered languages, and that anyone who spoke a language on the list could apply for a grant... merely because they were keeping the language alive by speaking it.

Excited at learning this information, the wise fool went online and made an application for an endangered language grant.

The first question on the form was the name of the language.

Thinking for a moment, Nasrudin wrote: Makak!

A few days later, he was invited to come for an interview at the UN's local Land of Fools field office.

When his turn came, he was led through to an interview

room, in which an official with a clipboard went over the details of his grant application.

'It says here, sir, that you speak a rare language called Makak… is that correct?'

Nasrudin shook his head.

'It's not *Makak*, but *Makak!* If you leave out the exclamation it makes no sense at all.'

'No sense in Makak!?'

'Yes, that's right.'

The interviewer was intrigued.

'Do you have any idea how many people speak Makak!?' he asked.

The wise fool thought for a moment, blinked, and said:

'Oh, just me, I suppose.'

'Just you?'

'Yes.'

'Well, that would make Makak! the most endangered language in the world.'

Nasrudin narrowed his eyes.

'Would the grant reflect the rarity of the language?'

The interviewer nodded eagerly.

'Think I can firmly say you'd get a huge grant. But, first, I need to ask a couple of basic questions.'

'Fire away,' said Nasrudin, as he imagined all the frivolities on which he would spend his wealth.

'Well,' the interviewer said, 'can you tell me some basic vocabulary in Makak!?'

Nasrudin gave a double thumbs up.

'Yes, of course.'

'Very well, I shall point to certain objects in this office and I'd like you to tell me how you say them in Makak!, OK?'

'Yes.'

'All right,' the interviewer said, pointing to a chair. 'What's the word for that?'

'Makak!' exclaimed Nasrudin.

'Hold on a moment,' the interviewer huffed. 'I thought you said Makak! was the name of the language.'

'Yes, it is.'

'And you mean to say it's also the word for "chair"?'

'Yes. They're both Makak!'

The interviewer scribbled a note on the clipboard and pointed to the table.

'That's Makak!' cried Nasrudin.

'Makak! as well?'

'Yes.'

'Remarkable.'

The interviewer pointed to the wall clock, the window, and a tree outside. Each time he pointed, the wise fool boomed:

'Makak!'

After an hour, the interviewer's patience was wearing thin.

'How can everything in your language be called the same thing?' he asked gruffly.

Looking at him sideways on, Nasrudin answered:

'Don't ask me... I only speak the damned language!'

Indiana Nasrudin

aving been weaned on the adventures of Indiana Jones, Nasrudin set out to make a name for himself by searching for the ancient lost city of Ubar.

The so-called 'Atlantis of the Sands' was said by many to lie beneath the vast Arabian Desert, the Empty Quarter. Through many months, the wise fool scoured its landscape, enduring extreme temperatures and terrible discomfort.

But at last, Nasrudin discovered the ruins of Ubar.

In jubilation, he danced around and around, punching both fists up into the air and thanking providence for revealing such a miracle to him.

Over the next weeks, he excavated the ruins alone.

Then, having taken a single photograph of the Atlantis of the Sands, he covered the ruins over once again.

When the photograph was published, the media begged the archaeologist to reveal exactly why he had decided to conceal the ruins.

The question was posed at a news conference, at which the wise fool was attended by camera crews from all corners of the world.

Taking a sip of water, he stared into space for a moment, before answering:

'Only a man who's discovered a lost city knows the sense of utter joy. It's like something from one's wildest dreams. And that was the reason I covered the ruins up and quietly tiptoed away.'

'I don't understand!' roared a journalist from *The New York Times*.

Nasrudin peered out at the sea of news media.

'I was simply setting the stage,' he said.

'Setting the stage for what?'

'For another dreamer such as myself to come along and find the ruins all over again.'

Thin Red Line

s an adventurer extraordinaire, Nasrudin left the Land of Fools and travelled to Kenya, where he was eager to go on safari.

Venturing from Nairobi, he travelled down into the Great Rift Valley, and then northwards in the direction of Samburuland.

After many hours of heat and dust, he spied a sign by the side of the road marking the equator. Having not crossed the equator before, he ordered the driver to stop, and leapt out to investigate.

It being the middle of nowhere, there wasn't anything of interest other than the sign. At least, that's what Nasrudin assumed.

For, as his eyes adjusted to the dazzling light, he noticed someone a short distance away. On all fours, it looked like a man digging something out of the ground.

Curious as to what it could be, the wise fool tramped over and introduced himself.

'I am Nasrudin from the Land of Fools,' he said, 'and this is my first time on the equator.'

The local stood up and dipped his head in greeting.

'It's a good year for it,' he said.

'A good year for what?'

'For the equator.'

'What d'you mean?'

The local frowned.

'Don't you know about the equator?' he asked.

'Know about it?'

'Yes.'

'What's there to know?'

'Well,' said the local, dusting the dirt from his front, 'it grows every year. And a few people like me come and cut away chunks.'

'What do you do with them?'

'We sell them as souvenirs,' the man said. 'And of course some people take them home and bury them.'

'Why ever would they do that?'

'Because when you bury pieces of the equator, they grow… even when you're not on the equator.'

The wise fool could hardly control his excitement.

'Could I see one of the chunks of equator?' he asked.

'Yes, of course,' said the local.

Treading back to the hole in which he had been digging, he pulled out a foot-long chunk of red tubing.

'Here's a piece I've just cut out.'

NASRUDIN IN THE LAND OF FOOLS

Nasrudin's eyes lit up. He imagined how even a small chunk of the equator would impress all the imbeciles in the teahouse back in the Land of Fools.

'Is it for sale?' he asked.

The local, a conman, nodded.

'The going rate is a hundred shillings an inch. This is about a foot, so I could let you have it for twelve hundred shillings.'

Nasrudin handed over his money and took possession of the precious piece of equator. He was about to walk back to the Land Rover when a thought struck him.

'If I'd want to grow this little piece of equator back home in the Land of Fools,' he said, 'are there any special instructions I should follow?'

The local smiled from the corner of his mouth.

'Make sure you bury it nice and deep,' he said.

'Anything else?'

'Yes…'

'What?'

'Remember that anyone who doubts it's a piece of the equator is proving themselves a fool.'

Nasrudin grimaced.

'I foresee problems ahead,' he groaned.

'And why is that?' asked the conman.

'Because I live in the Land of Fools.'

Living in Hope

fter much fanfare, the online retailer Amazon announced that they would start selling to the Land of Fools.

Right from the start, business boomed, as Foolslanders ordered an endless supply of useless objects.

Nasrudin, who had gained a reputation for never doing anything by halves, wondered how he could impress his neighbours and friends.

One day, when the other fools were receiving modest deliveries from Amazon, a vast convoy of trucks appeared over the horizon and rumbled towards the wise fool's home. One by one, the contents of each were unloaded. And, as it was, every fool in the neighbourhood watched.

'Whatever did you order?' one of the fools asked, his lower jaw hanging down.

'I ordered one of everything,' said Nasrudin.

The next day, another tremendous convoy arrived, and ferried every single item back to the warehouse.

Or, rather, almost every single item.

When an official from Amazon asked the wise fool to sign for the return of almost everything that had been ordered, he asked why only one object had been kept – a slim paperback book.

Holding a furry Persian cat close to his chest, Nasrudin raised an eyebrow.

'Naughty Fluffy here went online and ordered one of everything by mistake,' he explained. 'That's why I'm sending it all back. All except for this, the one thing Fluffy needs.'

The wise fool held up the book...

Computers For Cats.

King of the Cannibals

lthough in childhood he had exhibited no aptitude for the sciences, Nasrudin found himself gripped by a documentary one night – the story of an obscure cannibal tribe in the Pacific.

Despite trying to put the tribe and their eccentricities out of his mind, he couldn't stop thinking about them. So, resigning his low-wage job as a washer-upper in the teahouse, he signed on to learn anthropology.

Months passed, and then years, in which the wise fool dedicated himself to his studies.

The course was so challenging that most of the fools dropped out.

But, lured by his obsession for the cannibal tribe, Nasrudin persevered.

One fine summer day, he graduated, and set about funding an expedition to search for the tribe. Fortunately, a fool strode into the teahouse at that very moment, announcing how he had just won the Land of Fools Lottery.

He signed his winnings over to the name of science, and Nasrudin set off in a magnificent hot-air balloon.

Weeks passed in which the balloon, and the basket suspended beneath, were buffeted to and fro by the winds. Never once did Dr. Nasrudin ever consider giving up the challenge – not even when balloon and basket were flung high into the heavens, and then down into the ocean swell.

As luck would have it, the anthropologist was fished from the waves by none other than the cannibals with whom he was obsessed. Realizing that it was the beloved tribesmen who had saved him, he set about documenting their society and customs.

The first thing the tribe did was to fill a large pot with fresh water and light a fire under it. Next, they gathered herbs and berries from the jungle, and tossed them into the pot.

When the water was a good temperature, they lifted their guest ceremoniously into it.

'What kindly people they are!' Dr. Nasrudin exclaimed. 'For, grasping that I am battered and worn from my journey, they have prepared me a soothing aromatic bath!'

Little by little, the water grew hotter.

'How interesting!' Dr. Nasrudin called out. 'The tribe heat their baths to extraordinary temperatures!'

He was about to lie back in the water when a pair of warriors stepped forwards, their arms laden with the flesh of coconuts. With leering expressions, they threw the coconuts into the water.

'You are wonderful, wonderful people!' Dr. Nasrudin bawled. 'How good of you to feed me after my journey. Coconuts are my favourite delicacy of all!'

Clustering around, the tribal elders fanned the flames.

Vision blurred from the heat and smoke, the wise fool assumed the tribesmen were fanning him, rather than the fire below the pot.

'Remarkable! Remarkable!' he cried. 'The tribe's honouring of a guest is a thing of wonder! First, they saved me from the ocean. Then they bathed me in soothing water. After that, they fed me the succulent flesh of coconuts. As if that wasn't enough, they're now fanning me with palm fronds, as though I were their king!'

Greatly satisfied at having experienced the ritual, Dr. Nasrudin clambered from the pot. Ready for their lunch to be served, the tribe had formed an orderly column. At the head of the line was the chief, the royal sword of execution held between both hands.

'A guard of honour!' shrieked the wise fool in delight, as he thanked them. 'I am so touched, but this really isn't necessary!'

As the tribe watched in consternation, their prospective lunch stepped forwards to the potentate, took the regal sword from him, and waved it triumphantly above his head.

'When I get back to civilization, they won't believe that I, a humble anthropologist, was made King of the Cannibals!'

NASRUDIN IN THE LAND OF FOOLS

What the wise fool didn't know was that, in the culture of the island, he who held the sword of execution was regarded as ruler.

And so it was that the indefatigable anthropologist, Dr. Nasrudin of the Land of Fools, was crowned King of the Cannibals – a post he's believed to fulfil to this very day.

Relying on Ancestors

Nothing in the Land of Fools guaranteed success like pulling strings, which was rampant.

Indeed, it was the only way to be certain of getting ahead.

With a son as exceptionally dim-witted as his, the wise fool thanked providence that things were as they were. After an enormous amount of networking, he finally secured an interview at a leading firm for his eldest child.

But, as chance would have it, the interviewer appeared to be the one person in the Land of Fools who didn't turn a blind eye to pulling strings.

To Nasrudin's horror, she gave the young man an aptitude test.

Having accompanied his offspring to the interview, Nasrudin protested.

'I've used every contact I have and have left no string unpulled!' he barked. 'So there's surely no need for an aptitude test!'

The interviewer looked scandalized.

'How dare you admit to underhand ways!' she wailed.

'Of course I admit to it!' the wise fool cried back. 'After all, this *is* the Land of Fools, and nothing works better here than pulling a few strings!'

'Not in *this* firm!' the interviewer snapped. 'We prefer to rely on the reputation of our intelligence.'

Huffing and puffing, Nasrudin waved both fists in the air.

'Well, *I* prefer to rely on the kind of firm that relies on the reputation of one's ancestors!'

Hired and Fired

aving been brought up with exceptionally good manners, Nasrudin could never find the words with which to fire anyone.

This fact had never been a problem... until, that is, he was promoted in a government ministry within the Land of Fools.

However hard he tried, he couldn't bring himself to give anyone the sack.

One day, while in the bath, the wise fool had an idea – he would hire someone whose job it would be to fire anyone he wished.

Placing an advert, he was inundated with applications.

After a lengthy process of interviews, he found the perfect candidate – a young woman who was polite, well spoken, and had a proven track record in hiring and firing.

'You're hired,' said Nasrudin at the end of the interview.

The applicant gushed thanks.

'When do I start?' she asked.

The wise fool glanced at his watch.

'Immediately. That room across the hall will be your office, and your pay will be a thousand dinars a month.'

Again, the applicant cooed thanks.

'What will my first job be?' she asked earnestly.

Nasrudin thought for a moment.

'We don't have a budget to pay you,' he answered. 'So your first job is to fire yourself!'

Exchanging Conditions

Nasrudin had sunk into an abyss of depression, and spent day after day in bed.

A string of doctors was called and, one by one, they gave their diagnoses.

The first said the patient was in need of an enema.

The second affirmed he required fresh air.

The third intoned that a certain tonic was the only cure.

The fourth, a one-eyed hulk of a man, scribbled down a name and address.

'What's this?' the wise fool asked groggily.

'The details of a soothsayer who lives beyond the mountains.'

'What good is he to me?'

'Go meet him, and find out.'

Intrigued, Nasrudin scraped himself out of bed, put on his clothes, and tramped over the mountains, resting only when he reached a cave.

Holding the address up to the light, he called into the darkness.

'I've been told to come here,' he cried. 'To meet the soothsayer.'

A moment later, a wizened man emerged from the darkness.

'I am the soothsayer,' he said. 'What is it you need of me?'

When Nasrudin had explained his condition, the seer nodded.

'The reason for your malaise is that you're the reincarnation of Rameses III,' he explained.

The wise fool perked up, his eyes wide.

'Am I really?' he asked.

'Yes, yes, of course you are. It's the reason why you're so distressed. After all, no one is giving you the attention you deserve.'

In the blink of an eye, Nasrudin was a changed man.

Passing a coin to the soothsayer, he strode back over the mountains, and into the capital of the Land of Fools.

Within an hour or two he was in the teahouse.

Rather than the forlorn and wretched character they had all known, the wise fool was ebullient, throwing his weight around.

The landlord clenched both hands into fists.

'Who d'you think you are?!' he bawled.

'I am none other than the reincarnation of Rameses III!'

'Who on earth has led you to think such nonsense?'

'The soothsayer told me… the one who lives across the mountains.'

'And who sent you to him?'

'A doctor.'

'What doctor?'

'The towering hulk with a single eye.'

The landlord pointed to the corner.

'You mean him?'

Nasrudin turned, his eyes lighting up at seeing his saviour. Rushing over, he spewed thanks.

The landlord stomped over.

'How dare you send Nasrudin to the soothsayer in the cave?!' he snapped. 'Now he thinks he's Rameses III, and is causing problems for everyone.'

The doctor was peering out the window. Slowly, he turned to face the landlord.

'This morning he was lost in depression,' he said. 'And now, as you see, he's suffering from delusions of grandeur.'

'Exactly!' bellowed the landlord. 'Explain yourself!'

Sniffing, the doctor sipped his tea.

'I was simply exchanging one condition for another,' he said.

Fool's Block

Since earliest childhood, Nasrudin had wanted to be a writer.

But however hard he tried, he just couldn't get started on a novel, the one he knew was deep inside him.

One day, he overheard a pair of fools in the teahouse laughing about him.

It was the trigger he needed to get started.

Without wasting another moment, he bought a laptop and locked himself away.

Day and night he typed.

A month later, he emerged, the masterwork completed.

A month after that, the book was published to critical acclaim.

Invited on a TV chat show, he was asked what had got him started.

'I listened to fools,' he said.

'What's the story of the book?' the interviewer probed.

'It's the tale of a would-be novelist who can't think of what to write. So he writes a story about a would-be novelist who doesn't know what to write.'

The chat-show host signalled for applause.

As the tumultuous clapping died down, he posed another question:

'Is there going to be a sequel?'

Enlivened by all the attention, Nasrudin gave a double thumbs up.

'It's going to tell the tale of a would-be novelist who wrote a bestseller about being a would-be novelist, then admitted he was nothing but a halfwit writing for an audience of fools!'

Present vs. Future

Nasrudin was known throughout the Land of Fools as the worst-dressed man of all.

Years went by in which he didn't buy any new clothing.

When neighbours and friends offered him second-hand clothes, he shunned them, insisting that his threadbare clothing suited his outlook on life.

Even though the wise fool was so unpresentable, he had a good job in the Ministry of Cats and Dogs. And, as the years passed, he amassed a fortune in money which might have been spent on clothing and other luxuries.

Towards the end of his life, Nasrudin commissioned the very best portrait painter in the kingdom to paint him, and the very best writer to detail his life in a biography.

Before starting work on their commissions, Nasrudin asked for a certain level of fantasy.

To the artist, he said: 'I want you to depict me in a fabulous costume, surrounded by expensive décor and goods.'

To the writer, he said: 'I want you to depict me as the most generous and regal of men, the kind that others yearn to be.'

The wise fool's neighbour happened to be present, and was intrigued by the orders given. He asked Nasrudin why he was at last spending such an enormous amount on being commemorated in paint and words, when he could have used the money more aptly during his long and ill-dressed life.

Nasrudin shrugged.

'Had I spent my funds on being well-presented in life,' he said, 'I would have been soon forgotten. But, spending them to be well-presented in death, my legacy shall endure for centuries to come!'

Comparisons

U nable to get any other work, the wise fool took a job as a pack mule.

Each morning, laden with boxes and bales, he was forced to carry the loads up the mountain and over the desert.

Whenever he paused for a moment, he was whipped.

One night, unable to deal with the terrible conditions any longer, he whispered to the other pack mules:

'Let us rise up against our oppressors!'

The other pack mules – all of which were actual mules – remained silent.

Incensed that the others would not rise to the call for change, Nasrudin grimaced.

'I took this job as a pack mule because my life was so wretched,' he quipped. 'But, compared with this, I was living a life of luxury without knowing it. I only realize it now that I'm making comparisons!'

Timelines

ne afternoon, while walking along the riverbank, Nasrudin spotted the most beautiful little red flower he had ever seen.

Resisting the urge to pick it, he sat down beside it and stared in wonder and awe, amazed that nature could have created such astonishing beauty.

The more he looked at the flower, the more he felt overcome with love.

By the end of the afternoon, he came to the conclusion that he was in love with the flower. All night, he tossed and turned in his bed, desperately hoping that the flower could live as long a life as he.

As soon as dawn had broken over the horizon, Nasrudin hurried back to the riverbank and crouched down beside the flower.

Day after day he sat there, his heart pounding with love.

And night after night, he tossed and turned in bed.

Eventually, the petals began falling from the little red flower.

Bereft, the wise fool struggled to cope.

'O Great Creator,' he whispered, 'how can you have blessed me with true love, but cursed me with such a different timeline?'

Reliable Results

Having solved a well-publicized crime, the wise fool was hired as a private detective.

In the months that followed, he solved one crime after another, even though none of the other detectives cracked anything at all.

Confused at their colleague's success, the other detectives stopped trying to solve cases, and started to watch Nasrudin. By following him in disguise, they realized he was inventing cases.

First, he would lay a trail of clues.

Then, he would pretend to find them, and solve the case.

Dragged before the chief private eye, he was ordered to explain himself.

Swallowing anxiously, Nasrudin winced.

'I cheated because the results were so much more reliable,' he said.

Streaks Ahead

The Land of Fools was not unused to odd behaviour.

But, when Nasrudin was seen wearing full scuba diving attire in the teahouse, someone asked what he was doing.

Sipping his tea, the wise fool scratched a thumbnail down the length of his nose.

'Well might you wonder,' he said. 'But I am simply ahead of the curve.'

Self-improvement

hile larking about with his little son, Nasrudin inadvertently swallowed his pocket watch.

At first he was alarmed.

But to his surprise, and the surprise of those around him, he was unaffected.

Indeed, the mishap had actually improved him. For, rather than being late, as was his way, the wise fool was miraculously punctual.

He couldn't be late even when he tried.

Within a week of the pocket watch being swallowed, fools across the kingdom were swallowing pocket watches as well, in the hope of being improved.

As for Nasrudin, he was rushed to hospital for emergency surgery, having gulped down a comb, a toothbrush, and a pair of reading glasses.

NASRUDIN IN THE LAND OF FOOLS

As the patient recovered from the operation, the surgeon enquired how such an assortment of objects had got into his stomach.

The wise fool smiled demurely.

'A humble bid for self-improvement,' he said.

Elementary

Nasrudin hurried into a hardware shop and started poking around.

While wandering the aisles, he overheard the owner of the establishment bragging to a customer how he sold the finest array of goods on sale in all Foolsland.

Being the busybody he was, the wise fool marched up to the shopkeeper.

'D'you sell leather and twine, cork, and polish?' he asked.

The shopkeeper nodded eagerly.

'A hundred kinds of each, sir.'

'Then why don't you make shoes, and sell them, too?!' snapped Nasrudin.

Foolish Genius

asrudin was in need of a job.

Having had no luck in finding one through honest means, he decided to resort to more devious methods. He bought some paint, nails, a brush, and a billboard. Then he made a huge sign, which he positioned in the middle of town.

It read:

FOR A GENIUS
FOLLOW
THE SIGNS

With the rest of the paint, he drew arrows from the billboard to the hovel on the south side of town where he lived.

Then he waited.

All day…

All night…

All week…

Not once was there a knock from a would-be disciple in search of a guru.

Sick to the back teeth of waiting, Nasrudin stormed through the town and made a beeline for the teahouse.

Over sweet tea he explained to the landlord how he had made a sign and a series of arrows, in the hope of luring some fools his way.

'That's strange,' the owner of the teahouse said.

'What is?' asked the wise fool.

'Well, one of our regulars here is being hailed as a saviour by every fool in town.'

'Who, where, what?' snapped Nasrudin.

The landlord pointed to the northern side of town.

'He lives out there... and claims to be the most foolish man ever to have been born.'

'*Damnation!*' Nasrudin barked.

'What's wrong?' the landlord asked.

'Well, this being the Land of Fools, they're not only incapable of following the signs, but they're in search of a genius who's an imbecile!'

Edible Reading

asrudin wrote a novel, which he published himself.

So certain was he that it would be a bestseller, he printed a million copies.

To his horror, not a single copy sold.

On the point of bankruptcy, he had to think fast.

While in the teahouse, he overheard one of the regulars moaning that his front door always blew shut.

Pulling out a copy of his book, he sold it to the man, hailing it as 'the best doorstop ever invented'.

Next day, he heard a pair of washerwomen complaining at the price of firewood.

Whipping out a couple of copies of the novel, he sold them, advertising them as 'the best firewood ever invented'.

Within a week, people across Foolsland were using the novel as everything from paperweights to bricks with which to build new homes.

The only thing the books were not being used for was reading.

Nasrudin was found counting his money in the teahouse by a friend.

'I've almost sold them all,' he gloated.

'What's next?' his friend asked.

Nasrudin thought for a moment.

'I'll write a sequel,' he said. 'It'll be new and improved.'

'How could you improve on the first book?'

'By making it edible.'

'A book that's food?'

The wise fool smiled demurely.

'Precisely.'

'D'you think people will like the way it tastes?'

Nasrudin the bestselling novelist narrowed his eyes.

'I am sure they will,' he replied. 'After all, anyone who uses literature as doorstops, firewood, and even as bricks, has the most questionable taste.'

King of the Octopuses

In his younger years, Nasrudin became a pearl diver, in a bid to make a fortune fast.

But even the most dim-witted Foolslanders swam deeper and longer than him.

Within a day or two of splashing about in the water, the wise fool was a laughing stock.

All night, Nasrudin paced up and down, doing his best to come up with a solution.

All of a sudden, he was hit by a brainwave.

That morning, when the other pearl divers were getting ready down at the jetty, Nasrudin turned up with a barrel. The successful divers clustered round, wondering what was inside.

As they watched, the wise fool pulled the lid off the barrel, grabbed a live octopus from the water, and tied it to his belt. Reaching in a second time, he fished out a second octopus, and after it, a third.

When six large octopuses were tied in position, Nasrudin waved to the other divers and leapt into the water.

Intrigued to know what was going on, the others jumped in, swam down, and watched in amazement.

Sitting cross-legged on the sea floor, the wise fool waited calmly as the octopuses swam about gathering up the oysters. Tentacles clutching dozens of them, they ferried the shells over to Nasrudin, who dropped them in his net.

Once in a while, the wise fool would motion with his hand, and an octopus would rush over, breathing a stream of air into his nose.

When the net was full, the octopuses swam back to Nasrudin, attached themselves to his belt, and propelled him effortlessly up to the surface.

Back on dry land, Nasrudin put his mollusc helpers back in the barrel, thanked them in a curious sign language, and checked the oysters for pearls.

The other divers clustered around again.

Aghast, they babbled questions – each asking how the wise fool had trained octopuses to work for him.

Having harvested fifty perfect pearls from the oysters, Nasrudin looked vacantly at the other divers.

'It was simple, really,' he said.

'Training octopuses is simple?!' one of the divers hissed.

Nasrudin shrugged.

'Yes, the training was simple,' he replied. 'At least, it was simple compared with the first thing I had to do.'

The divers clustered around all the more.

'What was that?' one asked.

'Well,' Nasrudin replied, 'first I had to become King of the Octopuses.'

Making Sure

Nasrudin was found in the forest by an aged woodcutter.

He couldn't understand what the wise fool was doing.

For Nasrudin had a pot of glue in one hand and a leaf in the other.

One at a time, he picked a dead leaf off the ground and glued it back onto the tree.

Curiosity piqued, the woodcutter wondered why anyone would ever want to glue dead leaves back onto the tree.

'That won't work,' he said, after a long pause.

'What won't work?'

'You can't glue leaves onto a tree when they've fallen,' the imbecile said.

'Why not?'

'Because they'll never start growing again.'

Nasrudin paused, looked up at the woodcutter, and said:

'Have you ever tried doing it?'

'No, of course not.'

'Then how can you be so sure it doesn't work?' quipped Nasrudin.

The Real Land of Fools

asrudin was appointed as ambassador to the Court of St. James, and found himself in the Land of Fools Embassy, in the plush surroundings of Belgrave Square.

Under his authority was an array of Foolslanders – each one more dim-witted than the last.

On the first day of his posting, the wise fool was invited to witness English culture, at a demonstration of 'Morris Dancing'.

On the second day, he was invited to a lunch and served a dish called 'toad-in-the-hole'.

On the third day, he was invited to a traditional 'wife-carrying' contest in the countryside.

On the fourth day, he was invited to the burning of a human effigy at a Guy Fawkes celebration.

On the fifth day, he was invited to play 'conkers' with a child in the street.

On the sixth day, he was invited to eat a deep-fried Mars bar.

On the seventh day, Nasrudin packed his bags and left for the Land of Fools.

Upon his arrival, he was debriefed at the Ministry for Foreign Affairs, and asked to explain himself.

Dazed from his short experience in Britain, the wise fool rubbed his eyes.

'We may be the butt of every joke, but we're imposters! And, as an ambassador, I am one of the worst imposters of all!'

The minister asked what the diplomat was ranting about.

Rubbing his eyes again, Nasrudin cried:

'We may be fools, but it's England that's the *real* Land of Fools!'

The Eagle Chick

Nasrudin had lost playing poker in the teahouse and didn't have the money to clear his debt.

He would have avoided the teahouse, as it was there that the card sharp he had lost to was usually to be found.

For a few days, the wise fool stayed away. But eventually he couldn't bear being separated from his favourite haunt. So, mustering his strength, he made his way to the teahouse and slunk inside.

As soon as he sat down, the card sharp demanded the debt be repaid.

A look of terror in his eyes, Nasrudin stretched out his arms, flapped his hands up and down, and squawked like a bird.

'I'm a little eagle!' he screeched. 'And I'm just doing what little eagles do in the morning – flap about and squawk.'

'You're not an eagle!' the card sharp snapped angrily.

'Yes, I am!' Nasrudin huffed.

'If you're an eagle, let's see you fly!'

'But eagle chicks can't fly,' Nasrudin answered.

'If you're an eagle,' the poker player continued, 'where are your talons and your sharp beak?'

Again, the wise fool huffed.

'I've told you already – I'm an eagle chick, and so my talons and beak haven't formed yet!'

By this point, the man owed the debt was furious.

'All right then,' he roared, 'if you're an eagle chick, where are your mother and father?'

Nasrudin huffed a third time.

Squawking as loudly as he could manage, he exclaimed:

'How can you expect me to know where they are? I'm just a little eagle chick, all lost and alone in this big, wide world!'

Two-wheeled Tool

asrudin brought back a bicycle from his travels. Remarkably, no one in the Land of Fools had ever seen a bicycle before.

Within minutes of him cycling into the capital, a huge crowd had gathered. Seeing a business opportunity, the wise fool set up the first cycle shop in the Land of Fools.

Orders came in thick and fast, and a day or two later, the first shipment of cycles arrived.

Fools from across the kingdom were thrilled to own shiny new bicycles. But unlike Nasrudin, who had learned to ride his bike, the Foolslanders turned their bikes upside down and spun the wheels round and round.

Gathering the new bicycle owners around him, Nasrudin implored them to learn how to ride.

Despite him showing them the art of balancing, they weren't interested.

The dealer from the next kingdom, who had supplied the cycles, called to check how the novice cyclists were getting on.

'Not so well,' Nasrudin explained. 'They have not yet grasped that the object we have supplied them is a tool. Instead, they recognize it as an object of curiosity, and nothing more than that.'

Equality in Baldness

ne night, Nasrudin dreamt he was a politician, and that everyone gave him the respect he had always craved.

So, the next morning, he went to the teahouse and asked the landlord how he might get into politics. Although he had no political experience, the landlord had met all kinds of people, and had travelled far and wide.

Without batting an eyelid, he replied:

'Originality.'

'*Originality*?'

'Yes, originality.'

'What about it?'

'That's what you need if you want to get into politics!'

A little more confused than he had been when he entered the teahouse, the wise fool traipsed out. All day long he wondered what would be an original idea with which to found his first political campaign.

Walking along, he spied an elderly man crouched at the side of the road. The man was as bald as an egg, but had a

106

single strand of hair growing from the crown of his head. With extraordinary expertise, he had wound the hair round and around, so as to give the appearance that he was less bald than he actually was.

Striding over, Nasrudin introduced himself.

'I am campaigning to be the mayor,' he said. 'And I am thinking of giving free wigs to everyone who needs them.'

The old man squinted at the stranger.

'So?'

'So… if I were to get into office, I'd make sure you got a lovely new wig. Would you like that?'

The old man grinned.

'Yes,' he said. 'I would. But…'

'But, *what*?'

'But if I was given a free wig, all the people who have hair of their own would get jealous.'

Nasrudin thought for a moment.

'Hmmm,' he mumbled as he thought, 'I shall pass a law that everyone who has hair of their own will have to have their heads shaved every week, whether they like it or not. And then we shall all be equal!'

'But what about the wigs? You promised us free wigs!' the old man cackled.

Standing tall, Nasrudin grinned the grin of a politician – a politician who had ready answers for the questions of ordinary folk.

'Then I shall pass another law,' he boomed in a grandiose tone, 'a law that states that everyone must wear wigs, whether they like it or not!'

Fooling the Fools

asrudin was traipsing through the capital of the Land of Fools when he spotted a gold coin lying on the ground in the main square.

Rather than pick it up, he rushed to a bench and surveyed the square, suspecting it was a trick.

To his surprise, there wasn't anyone around.

Instead of making a beeline back to the coin and scooping it up, the wise fool assumed that whoever had planted it was a trickster of extraordinary brilliance.

All day long, he sat on the bench and stared out at the coin, in the belief that sooner or later the trickster would reveal himself.

But no one passed, not even when dusk gave way to night.

Unable to leave, Nasrudin sat on the bench, staring at the coin.

Even though he was exhausted, he strained to keep his eyes open.

NASRUDIN IN THE LAND OF FOOLS

As dawn was breaking over the Land of Fools, a rat emerged from the sewers under the square and foraged about for something to eat. Spotting the gold coin, and assuming it was a delicious sweetmeat wrapped in foil, the creature snatched it in one paw and scurried back to the sewer.

Nasrudin watched from the bench.

Leaping to his feet, he sprinted to the grate into which the rat had disappeared with the coin.

'So it was you!' he yelled. 'I should have known you were the trickster who kept me up all night!'

There was silence from the sewer.

Undeterred, the wise fool got down on his hands and knees, and cupped both hands around his mouth.

'You may be king of the sewers,' he cried, 'but don't think you can trick us up here in the Land of Fools!'

Dreams in Reverse

One night, having gorged himself on spicy curry, Nasrudin dreamt of a huge, free-standing doorway in the shape of an interlocking octagon.

A favoured symbol known to him since childhood, it was alluring in the most magical way.

Although he had no idea what lay beyond, the wise fool was unable to ignore it.

Gripped by anticipation, he turned the handle and pushed the octagonal door open.

Stepping through, he found himself in a land in which everything was back to front.

Dawn was sunset, and sunset was dawn.

Birds flew backwards.

The people spoke gibberish, because their language was in reverse.

And everything and everyone was growing not older, but younger all the time.

At first, the wise fool was critical of the way things were in this new land.

But, as time passed, he began to see that a back-to-front world was far more appealing than the one he was from.

One afternoon, he spotted something familiar in the middle of a field – a huge, free-standing doorway in the shape of an interlocking octagon.

The only difference was that the portal and its pattern were reversed.

The great octagonal door slid open, and Nasrudin glimpsed his own land beyond it.

He was about to slip back through when the loud braying of a donkey shook the ground.

Before he knew it, Nasrudin was lying awake in bed.

Still marvelling at the dream, he opened the window and called down to his ever-faithful donkey:

'!esrever ni dnal a fo tmaerd I'

Looking up, the animal replied:

'?uoy dnatsrednu I tsal ta taht ti si woH'

'!rood lanogatco eht hguorht kcab og dluoc I erofeb pu em ekow uoy ,yeknod diputs uoy ,esuaceB'

Translation:

'I dreamt of a land in reverse!'

'How is it that at last I understand you?'

'Because, you stupid donkey, you woke me up before I could go back through the octagonal door!'

Unfooled by Fools

hrough a chain of unlikely events, Nasrudin was given his own chat show on Land of Fools TV.

Each week, he invited the zaniest buffoons he could find to appear and make fools of themselves – which, of course, came naturally to them all.

At first, viewer figures were tremendously high, and the wise fool was hailed as the greatest TV personality in the history of the Land of Fools.

But as time passed, ratings slipped.

Hoping to rectify the situation, Nasrudin scoured the Land of Fools for crazier and zanier imbeciles to feature. Despite him pulling out all the stops, the plan backfired badly.

Before he knew it, Nasrudin was being decried as a fraudster and a bore.

Fuming with ire, the show's producers gave the once-celebrated chat-show host the sack. Throwing himself at their feet, Nasrudin pleaded and begged for one last chance, which he was eventually given.

Rather than combing the teahouses for idiots as he had done until then, Nasrudin hastened to the frontier, and crossed into the Land of the Sensible and the Sane.

Once there, he made a beeline for the most popular café, where he explained his predicament. Weighing up the dilemma at hand, and intrigued to see the Land of Fools for themselves, half a dozen Sensible and Sane-landers accompanied the wise fool back across the border.

That very night, they appeared on the chat show.

The ratings surged, and were higher than at any time in the kingdom's history.

After the show, the owner of the channel asked what had prompted the genius idea to feature non-fools.

His celebrity status regained, Nasrudin replied:

'As diehard fools, fools aren't always fooled by fools.'

Counting One's Lashes

lthough having been born with few redeeming qualities, Nasrudin won a prize for being the happiest man living in the Land of Fools.

It wasn't long before he was invited to the palace to demonstrate his exceptional cheer to the king – widely regarded as the bitterest leader in the kingdom's long and inglorious history.

'Well,' snapped the monarch, reclining on his golden throne, 'let's see a demonstration of your damned happiness!'

Not wishing to displease the ruler through displaying his abundant joy at being in the palace, Nasrudin remained silent.

'Hurry up and say something, you idiot!' the royal vizier hissed. 'Or you'll be punished!'

The wise fool remained tight-lipped.

Enraged at having his precious time wasted, the king ordered Nasrudin to be given twenty lashes.

Hearing his fate, the wise fool jumped up and down in jubilation.

'What the hell are you so pleased about?!' growled the king.

'Because it's only twenty lashes!' cried Nasrudin.

'What d'you mean... *only*?'

'Well, Your Majesty, had I exclaimed my utter delight and joy at being here in the palace, I would have certainly been given forty lashes!'

The king thought for a moment.

'Forty lashes!' bellowed the king. 'Twenty for wasting royal time, and the same again... for expressing your joy!'

Half and Half

asrudin secured a seat for himself as a member of parliament, but he quickly grasped that corruption was crippling the business of government.

Standing to make his maiden speech, he waved a hand above his head.

'I should like to state on the record that half the members of this chamber are liars and thieves!' he bellowed.

The speaker ordered for the remark to be withdrawn.

'Parliamentary law decrees that such an insult is against the rules!'

Clearing his throat, Nasrudin thrust a hand above his head a second time, as he yelled:

'I should like to state on the record that half the members of this chamber are not liars and thieves!'

The Essence of Time

asrudin was absolutely obsessed with time, and how it worked.

For years he studied the laws of physics.

But the more he studied, the more baffled he became.

Late one night, he had an idea.

Rushing into the sitting room of his home, he yanked the clock off the mantlepiece and placed it on the table. Fetching his box of tools, he opened the clock up and took it apart piece by piece in a desperate hope to locate the essence of time.

Within a few minutes, the wise fool had amassed a jumbled assortment of screws, coils, and springs, but was no closer to understanding time itself.

'Time, my tormentor! How will I ever know you?' he cried.

Genius Fleas

travelling salesman, who'd journeyed to the Land of Fools in the hope of making some fast cash, approached Nasrudin in the local teahouse.

In his hands was an empty jam jar.

Standing at the wise fool's table, he held the jar to the light and cried out:

'Behave yourselves, you damned little creatures!'

Nasrudin frowned.

'Who are you talking to?' he probed.

'To the fleas in this jam jar,' the salesman replied.

'*Fleas*? I don't see any fleas.'

'Of course you don't, because they're very special fleas.'

His curiosity piqued, the wise fool shrugged.

'What makes them so special?' he asked.

'For one thing, they're dwarf fleas, which is the reason you can't see them. And for another, they're genius fleas.'

'I've never heard of dwarf fleas, let alone genius fleas,' countered Nasrudin.

'Of course you haven't, because it's the first time dwarf genius fleas have ever been put up for sale here in the Land of Fools. They have been so incredibly popular. I came here with a thousand jars of them, and these are the only ones I've got left.'

'How much are they selling for?' the wise fool asked.

'A thousand dinars.'

'A thousand dinars for something I can't see?!'

The salesman rolled his eyes.

'A small price to pay for being in the presence of such greatness.'

Although Nasrudin knew his wife would scold him for lavishing so much money on something so unnecessary, Nasrudin pulled out his wallet and paid up.

A moment later, the jam jar was in his hands, and the salesman was gone.

Holding the jar up to his face, the fleas' new owner tapped the glass.

'Now, you wretched little creatures!' he yelled. 'I've paid a top price for you, so if I have any trouble at all, I'll get very angry. D'you understand?!'

The dwarf fleas didn't respond.

Just then, another teahouse regular strode up.

'That's a nice jar you have there.'

'The jar is quite ordinary,' Nasrudin replied. 'It's what's in it that matters.'

'Looks empty to me,' muttered the local.

'*Hah*!' snapped the wise fool. 'It's far from empty.'

'What's in it, then?'

119

'Dwarf fleas... but no ordinary dwarf fleas. They're genius ones!'

The local gasped.

'What a pity!' he moaned despondently.

Nasrudin glowered.

'Why's it a pity that the dwarf fleas are geniuses?'

'Because,' intoned the regular, 'as this is the Land of Fools, genius fleas are the last thing we need!'

No Thief Zone

Crime had become so bad in the Land of Fools that Nasrudin was robbed time and again – often more than once in a single night.

Sick of the thievery, the wise fool enquired in the teahouse if others had also been targeted by thieves. Commiserating, each regular recounted how they had been robbed repeatedly as well.

'The thieves come in the night and break into my home!' cried one Foolslander.

'They took everything I own,' groaned another.

That night, Nasrudin pushed his bed out into the street, along with all his possessions.

Then, locking the front door of his house, he kicked off his slippers and got into bed.

Just before he drifted to sleep, the wise fool heard footsteps approaching.

He opened an eye.

'What are you doing sleeping out here in the street?' asked the passer-by.

Nasrudin yawned.

'Thieves break into all the houses as we sleep,' he said, 'but they never burgle the streets.'

The passer-by, who was in actual fact a thief heading for Nasrudin's home, applauded the sharp thinking.

Next morning the wise fool awoke in a ditch, having been relieved of his blanket, bed, and slippers in the night.

Seeding Soil

In the height of summer, Nasrudin travelled to the desert with a cart full of fresh, damp soil which he had dug up from his field.

Although in most other kingdoms people didn't live in the middle of the desert, in the Land of Fools they did. The Foolslanders who dwelt there were especially dim-witted.

It wasn't long before a trio of desert-dwelling fools trundled over.

Like all Foolslanders, they were curious by nature.

They watched as the wise fool unloaded the cart and started raking the fresh soil over a small patch of sand.

One of the fools spoke for the rest:

'What on earth are you doing, friend?' he asked.

Nasrudin rolled his eyes.

'The fact that you're fools of the first order is proved by the fact you are living out here in the desert,' he said. 'So I wouldn't expect you to understand what I am up to.'

'What *are* you up to?' asked a second fool, standing beside the first.

'I am simply spreading this soil over the sand so as to seed it.'

'But soil can't be "seeded",' said a third fool.

'Have you ever tried it?'

The trio of desert-dwelling fools shook their heads.

'Well,' quipped Nasrudin, 'I suggest you cease from critiquing others on matters in which you are inexperienced yourselves!'

Exercise-O-Cycle

Slothful by nature, Nasrudin got into the habit of eating a diet of fatty kebabs, and doing no exercise at all.

Every week, he grew heavier.

And every week, he grew more boastful, declaring in the teahouse how he planned to take up cycling and become a champion in the sport.

The point arrived at which the wise fool was so overweight he could hardly make it from his home to the teahouse – a distance of a few hundred yards.

As he staggered out of his front door one day, a bicycle salesman buttonholed him.

'I've just arrived from the Land of the Sensible and the Sane,' he said, 'and have brought with me this glorious new model of bicycle.'

The wise fool looked the salesman up and down, then did the same with the cycle.

'One wheel's far bigger than the other,' he said accusingly.

'Naturally,' countered the salesman. 'As I told you, it's a special new design.'

Unable to help himself, and eager to upstage the other Foolslanders at owning such an unusual contraption, Nasrudin bought it on the spot.

Clambering aboard, he soon realized that it took an enormous amount of effort to stay balanced, let alone go forwards. Well aware that the regulars in the teahouse would howl with laughter if they knew he had been conned, he practised in secret each night.

Within a week, Nasrudin could ride the bicycle perfectly. And, more importantly, the time and effort required had prevented him from lounging about in the teahouse.

Two weeks after purchasing the cycle, he not only had the body of an athlete, but also a sharp business idea.

The slimmed-down Nasrudin pedalled to the teahouse, where the other regulars admired him and his unusual contrivance – which he called an 'Exercise-O-Cycle'.

Ten minutes after his arrival, he had orders for fifty.

A few weeks after that, the wise fool was a millionaire.

Invited on a leading Foolsland chat show, he was asked for the secret of his success.

An Exercise-O-Cycle beside him, he turned to look into the camera.

'The secret of my success was to take what was provided and to use it to my advantage,' he said.

Rationing the Joy

hile walking into town one morning, Nasrudin spotted a discarded clock spring lying on the road.

Without thinking, he picked it up and began twanging the end as he walked.

The sound was pleasing not only to his ears, but to those of a farmer who was on his way to market with a cart full of melons.

'What do you want for that lovely instrument?' he asked.

The wise fool looked at the farmer, and at the melons.

'I'll swap it for one of those.'

The farmer agreed, and passed over the largest melon.

The melon was so heavy that Nasrudin found it hard to carry into town. Cursing himself for being so stupid as to swap the clock spring, he put the melon on the ground and rested.

Standing there, he had an idea.

If he took off his turban, and tied it in a certain way, he could make a kind of harness for the melon. A moment or two later, the melon was nicely trussed up, and was being carried easily into the town.

In the bazaar, a crowd gathered at seeing such an unusual melon-harness.

One of the traders hurried up.

'I'll swap the secret of the technology for a field I own outside the city!' he gasped.

Bewildered that his turban would be of interest to anyone at all, the wise fool took the land deed for the field. Then, handing over his turban, he explained the system of knots he had used to make the melon-harness.

With no way to carry the melon, he divided it, and handed out chunks of the fruit to anyone who wanted them.

That afternoon, Nasrudin went to inspect the field that he had swapped for his turban. To his sorrow, he found the land had squatters.

On the advice of a friend, he took the ownership deeds to a lawyer in the bazaar, but was informed that the deeds were worthless.

The wise fool was about to trudge back home when a stranger approached him.

'Are you not the kind-hearted man who gave me a piece of the most delicious melon this morning?' he asked.

Nodding, Nasrudin explained the highs and lows of the day.

Although not wishing to pry, the stranger probed if he might have a look at the land documents. Having had an opportunity to look through the papers, he put them back in their envelope.

'They do appear to be of little value,' he said. 'But the same cannot be said for that…'

The stranger tapped a fingertip to the postage stamp on the envelope.

'By trade I'm a philatelist,' he said. 'In other circumstances I might have thought to have taken advantage of you, but you were kind enough to feed me without knowing who I am.'

Nasrudin frowned.

'What about the stamp?'

'It's an Inverted Red from the Land of Old and New, the rarest of the rare stamps in all existence!'

'How much is it worth?'

The philatelist shrugged.

'At least a million dinars!'

Nasrudin expressed thanks for the information. Amused by the day's sequence of events, he trudged home.

Reaching the spot at which he had found the clock spring that morning, he peeled the postage stamp off the envelope, and spoke to it:

'Listen to me, you little Inverted Red from the Land of Old and New,' he said, 'I've had far more than my share of unexpected joy for the day, so I'm going to leave you here for someone else to find.'

With that, Nasrudin placed the little postage stamp squarely in the dirt, and wandered solemnly home to bed.

Sensible Day

very single day in the Land of Fools was April Fool's Day – all except for 1st April, which was known as Sensible Day.

On Sensible Day, Foolslanders played tricks on one another, howling with laughter at pranks made through sensible behaviour.

Invariably, Nasrudin fell victim to endless Sensible Day pranks, a point which frustrated him no end.

One year, unable to stand it any longer, he locked himself in his house before 1st April came around.

Having had such fun with him in previous years, the Foolslanders from the teahouse turned up at the wise fool's house.

One at a time, they banged on the windows and yelled sensible comments.

'The sky is really blue and not brown!' one shouted.

'Sheep really do have coats of wool, and not straw!' called another.

'And your house is really made from bricks, rather than snow!' bawled another.

The banging and the yelling went on for hours, with more and more fools turning up to join in the fun.

With the full moon high overhead, Nasrudin opened the door to his house and begged the Foolslanders to stop.

'If I was capable of living in a sensible world,' he moaned, 'I would leave the Land of Fools and never return!'

Bull-speak

Having fallen in love, Nasrudin learned that the object of his affection regarded bullfighters as the bravest and most handsome men alive.

Although terribly fearful of bulls, and horrified by the barbaric sport, the wise fool considered taking lessons as a matador. Hopelessly in love, he made his way to the bullring, and watched as one courageous young man after another was gored.

Crestfallen, Nasrudin was about to leave when he spotted the girl under whose spell he had fallen seated in the front row. Like everyone else in attendance, she had been caught up in the frenzy of excitement.

Seizing the moment, the wise fool hurried to the pen in which a colossal and ferocious bull was scraping a hoof to the ground before being let into the ring.

Cupping both hands around his mouth, he called through the bars:

'Listen to me! My beloved is sitting out there!' he cried. 'As you can probably tell, I'm no matador. I'm just pretending. So, when they let you out, please play along with me, and remember that I'm just pretending!'

Nasrudin leapt over the bars and strode purposefully out into the middle of the ring.

A second after that, the bull was charging at him, huffing and puffing with ire.

As it charged, the wise fool gave the animal a wink.

The next thing Nasrudin knew, the bull's horn had torn into him.

'How stupid I am!' he wailed, as he was rushed away on a stretcher. 'I ought to have translated my plea into bull-speak!'

Actions and Words

Nasrudin's neighbour bought a pitbull, which attacked anyone who walked by his house.

As the wise fool was continually passing, he was continually attacked.

Despite liking dogs, the point came when enough was enough.

'Please tie up your animal,' he said to the neighbour. 'As you can see from my wounds, I've been attacked time and again.'

The neighbour rolled his eyes.

'To hell with you!' he yelled.

In the days that followed, the pitbull grew all the more ferocious. Having been bitten all over, Nasrudin took matters into his own hands.

He bought a dozen steak knives, thirty six-inch nails, and a spiked collar for a dog.

Putting the collar around his neck, he punched the nails through a leather face mask and strapped it into place, and tied a steak knife to each finger.

Lowering himself down onto all fours, he waited for his neighbour to come home.

When the man eventually appeared, Nasrudin struck, stabbing and clawing in an horrific attack.

Begging for mercy, the neighbour demanded to know what was going on.

Still on all fours, Nasrudin exclaimed:

'I'm merely demonstrating in actions what you apparently did not understand in words!'

Peacock Calm

Nasrudin was so anxious by nature that he started seeing a therapist once a week.

Although the patient was making good progress, the analyst suggested that the wise fool get himself a pet which would afford him a sense of calm in high stress situations.

'A pet bird is the very best creature to provide tranquillity,' he said.

Giving thanks, Nasrudin left the clinic and made his way home.

On the way, he spotted a man at the side of the road, holding a box.

Ever curious, the wise fool asked what was inside.

'A lovely little peacock chick,' the man said. 'I'm taking it to the market to sell.'

Remembering the analyst's suggestion that he get himself a pet bird, Nasrudin bought the creature on the spot.

Within a week or two, the chick had sprouted from a fledgling to a fully grown peacock.

The creature squawked all night, and attacked anyone who went near it.

Anyone, that is, except for Nasrudin.

The bird and its owner became inseparable. Better still, Nasrudin was no longer filled tip to toe with angst.

So long as the peacock was beside him, the wise fool was as calm as a cucumber.

Having been unable to fly in an aeroplane on account of his nerves, Nasrudin was now so calm that he decided to travel to the Land of the Sensible and the Sane by plane.

He bought a ticket for himself, and one for the enormous bird.

The pair of them boarded, and the flight took off.

But as soon as they were airborne, the peacock went crazy – flapping wildly and attacking anyone who got close.

Despite the mayhem all around, the wise fool was perfectly calm.

Things got so bad that the captain emerged from the cockpit to see what was going on.

'How on earth could you bring that terrifying creature on the flight?!' the captain wailed in utter consternation.

Stroking a hand lovingly over the bird's tail feathers, Nasrudin replied:

'One man's terror is another man's calm.'

Tears of God

own on his luck, Nasrudin was found selling small glass bottles filled with clear liquid.

'What's in them?' a fool outside the teahouse asked.

'Tears of God.'

The fool's face lit up.

'Are they *real* tears of God?'

The wise fool nodded.

'Then I'll take one,' said the fool, handing over a coin.

By evening, Nasrudin had made enough money selling Tears of God to buy a sumptuous feast not only for himself, but for his best friend.

Towards the end of the meal, the friend asked what had been in the bottles.

'Tears of God.'

'And what are they?'

Nasrudin smiled.

'Rainwater.'

'How can you have the shame to sell such a thing?' asked the friend.

'If Foolslanders are stupid enough to buy bottles filled with Tears of God,' retorted Nasrudin, 'then who am I to deprive them of their belief?'

Important Details

n one of the rare occasions that Nasrudin had good luck, he won the Land of Fools Lottery.

In a bid to be seen as the most generous man in the kingdom, he announced that he would spend the money on building the finest soccer field and stadium the kingdom had ever known.

In the weeks that followed, he bought a piece of land on the edge of the capital and had a perfect pitch laid, with gleaming stands constructed for all the fans. He built an avenue of magnificent palms, laid on free luxury buses, and gave every fool a complimentary season ticket.

Within weeks of winning the lottery, Nasrudin had spent every penny.

At last, the evening of the first fixture arrived.

Borne to the stadium in their luxury buses, the fans were provided free refreshments and ushered to their seats. The players strolled out of the tunnel onto the pitch to tumultuous applause.

Once they had taken their positions, the referee blew the whistle.

But the players didn't move.

Having spent every penny on the stadium, the pitch, and on everything else, Nasrudin hadn't anything left with which to buy a ball.

Hard Times in Fairyland

When Nasrudin's little son lost a tooth, he put it under his pillow.

Next morning, having found an old carrot where he'd expected to find chocolate, he complained to his father.

'I hear that the Tooth Fairy's going through hard times,' the wise fool explained.

'What kind of hard times, Baba?'

'Apparently there are such hard times in fairyland that the Easter Bunny has had to double up as the Tooth Fairy.'

'But why have I only been left a horrid old carrot, instead of the chocolate the Tooth Fairy and the Easter Bunny usually bring?'

'As I told you, these are hard times. I hear that the poor old Easter Bunny can't afford chocolate. As well as putting second-rate carrots under your pillow, he's had to get a job washing dishes at the teahouse… and he's totally fed up!'

'D'you see him there, Baba?'

'Where?'

'At the teahouse, when you go there to wash up?'

Nasrudin nodded to his son.

'The Easter Bunny and me are old friends,' he said.

'Baba... is that why you know how fed up he is?'

'Yes.'

'You're so lucky knowing the Easter Bunny so well! I wish I could meet him.'

Nasrudin glanced down at his little son again, his eyes welling with tears.

'Don't worry about that,' he whispered. 'With the fullness of time, you're destined to be introduced.'

Danger: Potholes!

The roads in the Land of Fools were so riddled with potholes that a special commission was established to deal with them.

A panel of councillors, led by Nasrudin, agreed to hire a team of workers to fill in the potholes and repair the roads.

The only problem was that there was no budget available to pay any salaries.

As a gesture of goodwill, the wise fool volunteered to spend his free time repairing the roads himself. But there were so many holes that he soon realized there was no hope of accomplishing the task.

So, begging and borrowing some wooden planks, paint, and nails, he made a clutch of signs, which read:

DANGER: POTHOLES!

Having hit another car as he swerved to miss one of the signs, an enraged Foolslander demanded to know why the council didn't repair the potholes instead of putting up signs.

Irked at being reprimanded while working as a volunteer, Nasrudin glowered at the motorist.

'Why solve a problem when, with a little training, you can learn to live with it?'

Never Lost Again

Famed for having no sense of direction, Nasrudin had a compass tattooed prominently on the back of his right hand.

'As you know, I used to get lost all the time,' he told a friend in the teahouse, 'but now all I have to do is to glance at my hand like this and see where north is.'

'What happens when you want to go south?' asked the friend.

'Then I follow the compass on my other hand.'

'What if you want to go west?'

The wise fool stuck out his right foot.

'Then I follow this compass.'

'And what happens when you want to go east?' the Foolslander asked.

'Simple,' said the wise fool, 'if I need to go east, I follow the compass on my left foot.'

'But I thought you couldn't tell left from right?'

'That's true, I can't,' sighed Nasrudin. 'But I'll get to that once I've solved the problem of having no sense of direction.'

Damned Either Way

asrudin was banned from the teahouse for a month for lying.

Bereft, as he loved the establishment, he fell into a state of terrible despair.

As he languished at home in sorrow and shame, he had an idea.

Dressing up as a circus clown, he strode through the doors of the teahouse.

'Hey! Wait!' cried the doorman. 'Aren't you Nasrudin?!'

'No,' said the clown.

'Yes, you are! And you're lying again! That means a two-month ban!'

The wise fool huffed.

'All right! All right! Ask me again!'

Taking pity, the doorman posed the question a second time.

'Are you Nasrudin?'

'Yes! I am. I am. I am!' wailed Nasrudin, pulling off his disguise.

'Well, you're banned for lying. Get out!'

The wise fool stamped his feet.

'You can't win in this place!' he roared. 'You're damned if you lie, and damned if you don't.'

Not As I Am

Nasrudin got a job as a life coach.

Recruiting the services of the very best signwriter in the Land of Fools, he had an exquisite sign made, which read:

LIFE COACHING
FROM THE MASTER

To the wise fool's surprise, not a single person was lured by the sign.

Bewildered at how his career as a life coach was going, the wise fool repaired to the teahouse.

'Saw your sign,' said one of the locals.

'Why didn't you come and ask for some life coaching?'

The local frowned.

'Well, you're a well-known failure,' he said. 'It's the reason you've set yourself up as a life coach.'

His face flushing, Nasrudin clenched a fist and waved it at the other regular.

'Don't be as I am, but be as I'll tell you to be!'

Tomorrow's Me

Nasrudin had a dream that he had somehow stepped through a portal into tomorrow.

Befuddled, he peered out the front door of his house.

The postman, who was passing, called out greetings.

'How do you know it's me?' quipped Nasrudin.

'I know it's you, because you're Nasrudin.'

The wise fool shook his head.

'No, no, no,' he said. 'You know me from yesterday. But I'm the me from tomorrow. And you've never met the tomorrow me before.'

One or the Other

aving found work as a tailor, Nasrudin won a cruise at the Tailors' Annual Ball.

Although he disliked being at sea, he calmed himself with the knowledge that huge ships rarely sink. Dressing up in his finest clothes, he boarded the vessel.

On the second day, the ship hit an iceberg and sank.

Miraculously, the wise fool was the only passenger who managed to scramble into a lifeboat. Thankful to be alive, he raised the sail and lay back as the little boat seemed to steer itself towards the horizon.

Days passed, and Nasrudin grew increasingly cold. He found himself wishing he had some cloth and tools so that he could make a warm jacket.

Leaning back, he spotted a huge white sheet of canvas – the exact material he needed.

Rummaging around in the boat's supplies, he found a sharp knife, fishing hooks, and line. Within a day or two he had made the most wonderful jacket.

The only problem was that, with no sail, the lifeboat was becalmed.

Throwing his head back, he called up at the endless blue sky:

'O Great Creator! Why in life is it all about having one thing or the other?!'

Genius Machine

Nasrudin invented a device to turn fools into geniuses, and geniuses into fools.

As word of the machine spread, Foolslanders hurried to the capital and stood in line.

Paying their money, some of the dimmest fools in existence became geniuses in the blink of an eye.

But one at a time, the geniuses queued up again, to be turned back into fools.

Nasrudin asked one of them why he wanted to be turned back.

'I always wanted to be a genius,' he said, 'but now I have experienced it, I realize it's so much less exhausting to go through life as a fool.'

Stay Calm and Carry On

asrudin was strolling through the capital of the Land of Fools one bright afternoon when he spotted the sky being reflected in a gleaming glass and steel building.

Assuming that the sky had somehow become trapped in the skyscraper, he ran through the streets, drawing the marvel to the attention of others.

Within a few minutes, a crowd of Foolslanders had gathered at the foot of the building.

'Stay calm and carry on!' Nasrudin bellowed at the top of his lungs.

'How can you tell us to stay calm when you are frantic?' snapped a young man at the back.

'Of course I'm frantic!' the wise fool riposted angrily. 'You would be, too, if you'd discovered the sky getting caught up in a building like that!'

Extra for Free

asrudin set himself up as a barber but, since he only had a razor, he shaved the heads of all the customers whether they liked it or not.

Within a day or two no one turned up, as word had spread.

Retreating to the teahouse, the wise fool gave voice to his woes.

'If a baker gave you extra bread for free, you'd be happy wouldn't you?' he asked.

The landlord nodded.

'And if a butcher gave you a pound of sausages for nothing, you'd be happy, too?'

Again, the landlord nodded.

'Well,' said Nasrudin on reflection, 'all I was doing was giving them a little extra for free.'

Counting One's Blessings

asrudin wondered why the sun didn't switch places with the moon, and the moon switch places with the sun.

He mentioned the idea in the teahouse, and a handful of regulars spoke up, saying they thought it was a sensible idea. So, with far too much time on his hands, the wise fool drew up a petition to swap the moon with the sun, and the sun with the moon.

But when it came down to it, no one supported the idea.

Bewildered at the lack of backing, Nasrudin climbed onto his roof just before sunset, gazing up at the last strains of sunlight and the crescent moon.

'You two should count your blessings!' he hollered. 'If I was anywhere but the Land of Fools I'd have got the support needed to have you both switched around!'

Stands to Reason

aving lost the key to his house, Nasrudin was in a rotten mood.

Even though he lived across the street from a locksmith, he refused to have another key cut.

Instead, he set about changing the system. The way he saw it, if there were no thieves, then there would be no need for locks and keys.

Watching from across the street, the neighbour asked the wise fool why he simply just didn't get a new key and leave it at that.

Regarding the locksmith with a venomous stare, Nasrudin replied:

'The fact that I have lost my key stems from the fact we need locks because of the thieves. But if there were no thieves, we would need no locks. And if we had no locks, it would stand to reason that we would have no use for keys.'

Part-time Treasure

 asrudin had a dream that there was a treasure vault beneath his house, and that it was reached through a trap door.

On waking, he searched for a secret entrance.

To his amazement and delight, he found that there was one, just as it had appeared in the dream. Opening it, the wise fool discovered a passageway, and a chamber filled with a golden treasure.

Standing guard was a jinn, which hailed Nasrudin.

'You are my master and this is your treasure,' the jinn boomed. 'Should I transport it to the surface, so that you can buy what you wish?'

The wise fool was about to agree, when something occurred to him.

'I am the laziest person I know,' he said. 'If I were to have a treasure like this, I'd surely get all the lazier.'

The jinn frowned.

'Should I make the treasure vanish then, master?' he asked.

Nasrudin swallowed hard at the thought. After all, the treasure was a figment plucked from his wildest dreams.

'Could I ask for a compromise?'

Again, the jinn frowned.

'What kind of compromise, master?'

'Well,' said Nasrudin, 'can you make it disappear half the week, and reappear for the other half? That way, there'll still be hope for me.'

Pet Melon Business

ven though he was living in the Land of Fools, Nasrudin had a pet melon, which afforded him a great deal of attention.

People would venture from across the kingdom to see the pet melon. They would shower it with gifts. They would pay to have their picture taken with the pet melon, and would buy all manner of souvenirs commemorating their visit, which the wise fool sold them.

One day in the teahouse, the landlord asked when Nasrudin would grow up and start a proper business.

'My dear friend,' answered the wise fool curtly, 'I already have a thriving business. I'm in the pet melon business.'

Bare Essentials

Nasrudin was flat broke, having made a series of bad investments.

With no more than a few coins to his name, he went to the teahouse and ordered a simple bowl of chicken soup.

The next day, with even less money to his name, he asked for chicken soup without the chicken. When it was served, he sat there, spoon in hand, eyes closed.

The landlord asked if there was something wrong with the soup.

'Not at all,' the wise fool answered. 'I am simply imagining that this bowl of soup is a magnificent meal fit for a king.'

Next day, yet more impoverished, Nasrudin ordered half a bowl of the chickenless soup.

The day after that, he asked for a single spoon of the soup.

Concerned that Nasrudin was making a mockery of his establishment, the landlord demanded an update.

'When my imagination was lacking,' he explained, 'I needed a full portion of good soup. But now that my imagination is much better, I can make do with the bare essentials.'

The landlord shrugged.

'Surely your stomach realizes it's getting almost nothing to eat?'

'*Hush*!' quipped Nasrudin. 'The last thing I need is for my stomach to talk to my brain!'

Not So Sacred

The king put Nasrudin in charge of the sacred spring in the Land of Fools.

Fools would turn up from across the kingdom bearing bottles, which the wise fool would dutifully fill for them. Even the most disconsolate Foolslanders had their spirits revived by taking a sip of the sacred water.

A few weeks after being given the position as guardian of the sacred spring, Nasrudin turned up for work early one morning to find that the source had run dry due to drought.

Filled with fear, the wise fool ran a hose from a standpipe, and replenished the source.

When the fools began to arrive, each of them clutching an empty vessel, they had it filled by a beaming Nasrudin. Each morning, the wise fool would get to work a little earlier than usual in order to replenish the spring.

All went well until one morning, when a menial official spotted the deception.

Furious, he accosted the guardian, demanding to know why ordinary water was being used to top up the sacred spring.

'You have seen, have you not,' said Nasrudin, 'how ecstatic the Foolslanders are at receiving the water?'

Still fuming, the official cocked his head downwards in a nod.

'They seem happy, but it's because you're tricking them!' he roared.

The wise fool sniffed.

'Who am I, a humble servant of the sacred spring, to separate the good people of the Land of Fools from the little joy they most certainly deserve?'

Polar Painting by Numbers

 asrudin started painting by numbers and, like everything he did, he did it on a vast and uncompromising scale.

One evening, he watched a nature documentary about the Arctic. The infinite white emptiness caught his attention. However hard he tried, he couldn't get it out of his mind.

Packing brushes and a crate of colourful paints, he was dropped by parachute onto the frozen tundra.

As soon as he had collided with the ice, the wise fool freed himself from the harness. Then, having opened the paints, he numbered the parts of the parachute, and filled them in with colour.

After that, he coloured in his snow-suit, skis, and backpack.

Over many weeks, the wise fool numbered the windswept white landscape, filling it in with colour a little at a time. Each night he would radio back to the headquarters in the Land of Fools to say he was safe.

One morning he reached a cave, and radioed to base that he was going to proceed inside. It was the last call from the intrepid painting-by-numbers-crazed explorer.

As Nasrudin was a national hero by this point, the king ordered a pair of imbeciles from the royal court to go and search for him. For weeks the rescue team tracked the eccentric artist by following the trail of colour… a trail of colour that ended at the cave from which Nasrudin had made his final call to base.

Curled up asleep at the back of the cave was a polar bear.

The pair of Foolslanders sent on the rescue mission approached. Holding up a lamp, they saw that the animal was covered in a kaleidoscope of colours.

'He's been here all right!' the first imbecile cried.

Woken from its slumber, the polar bear rose up, baring its fangs.

'Oh my goodness!' the first imbecile exclaimed. 'Its tongue is blue!'

The second imbecile let out a shriek.

'Not content with painting the animal's body, Nasrudin must have gone inside, and painted that as well!'

Knitted Fiction

Nasrudin had always wanted to be a writer but had no idea where to start.

While in the teahouse one day, he overheard a musician explaining how he derived inspiration from his surroundings. The comment was exactly what the wise fool needed.

Abandoning his job at the sacred spring, he bought a ream of paper and started writing an epic novel by hand. He filled the first few pages with a description of his home. Once he had described it, he stared into a full-length mirror on the wall, and wrote about the reflection. The storyline was built around the trials and tribulations of a would-be writer, and the private agonies he endured in the name of his art.

After many weeks, Nasrudin wrote the final page.

Despite the odds stacked against him, he found a publisher right away, and the novel became a runaway success.

Invited on a TV chat show, he was asked what he was working on.

'It's a project about a writer who drew inspiration from his surroundings,' he explained, 'but then realized he was an absolute fake.'

Leaning forwards with interest, the chat-show host asked whether the wise fool was typing the book or writing it by hand.

'Neither,' he replied.

'Then you're dictating it?'

'Wrong again.'

'Perhaps you could elucidate for us the nature of your method,' probed the host obsequiously.

'I am knitting the story,' Nasrudin said.

'*Knitting* it?!'

'Yes. In pink alpaca wool.'

'But that is the most preposterous thing I've ever heard!'

'Surely no more preposterous than fooling fools with nonsense they don't understand,' he said.

Follow the Leader

asrudin watched a documentary about Andy Warhol, and came to understand how the revered pop culture artist created his mass media following for himself.

Warhol, the documentary explained, had hired a film crew to tail him, and a second film crew to follow the first one.

Inspired by the example, Nasrudin did the same.

He hired a film crew to follow him, and another film crew to follow the first one.

Then, he hired a third crew to follow the second, and a fourth to follow the third.

On and on it went, until every film crew in the Land of Fools was following one another in a great snaking line of self-serving publicity.

Eventually his assistant informed him there were no film crews left to hire.

Furious at hearing the news, the wise fool picked up his own camera and rushed after the last film crew in the chain.

'I've got to hurry!' he called as he went. 'I happen to know that I'm going to do some crazy things tonight!'

Stone Home

hile looking through the Land of Fools eBay pages one afternoon, Nasrudin spotted an advertisement:

Pet Dragon Fledgling For Sale
Loveable and fully house-trained
Needs cuddles and love
Buyer must collect

Excited at the thought of such an unusual pet with which to wow his friends, the wise fool made contact with the seller and set off to the collection address.

Travelling for days across deserts and through forests, he eventually arrived at a castle perched atop a jagged line of crags. Once he had made it known that he was there to pick up a dragon fledgling, he was led around to the stables.

In a room scorched by flame, he set eyes on the kindest little dragon fledgling he had ever seen. Indeed, it was the one and only dragon fledgling he had ever seen.

NASRUDIN IN THE LAND OF FOOLS

The fledgling was put into a shoebox with air holes punctured on the sides. Nasrudin paid the fee, put the box under his arm, and began the long journey home.

Right from the start the dragon fledgling began making his presence known.

No sooner had the pair of them climbed down from the castle than the pet dragon began squawking for food.

Uncertain what baby dragons lived on, Nasrudin did his best to find something suitable in the forest, which they were zigzagging through. It turned out that the fledgling adored gorging himself on woodlice.

Once contented, he climbed back into his shoebox, and the two travellers continued on their journey.

A little further on, the dragon fledgling started squawking again.

Grumbling at having no peace and quiet, Nasrudin opened the box. The creature's great doleful eyes stared up at him and blinked.

'You want a cuddle, don't you?' sighed the wise fool.

So, as they crossed the endless sand desert, Nasrudin cuddled the dragon fledgling, regaling it with nursery rhymes.

As they approached the capital of the Land of Fools, they put up at a quaint wooden guest house for the night. The wise fool arranged for a bowl of succulent woodlice to be brought for his pet, which the little dragon devoured.

The pair of travellers snuggled up for the night in a four-poster bed.

Nasrudin drifted into sleep, his mind racing with images of he and his beloved fledgling living together in bliss.

Alas, the dreamscape came to a sudden end.

The wise fool awoke to find the guest house on fire.

Struggling to make sense of what had occurred, he realized that the dragon fledgling had sneezed in his sleep, setting fire to the curtains.

Next morning, Nasrudin posted on eBay:

Used Pet Dragon Fledgling For Sale!
Loveable and fully house-trained.
Needs cuddles, love, and
a home made of stone.

End Game King

 espite being largely good for nothing, Nasrudin was found to have an extraordinary ability in playing championship chess.

Having been signed up for the chess circuit at a tender age, the wise fool trounced one opponent after the next with an extraordinarily aggressive style.

He didn't believe in developing his pieces, but went straight in for the kill.

The flair for ferocious attacks earnt Nasrudin the nickname 'The End Game King'.

While pausing between bouts during a tour in the Land of the Moody and the Meek, the wise fool agreed to give an interview to a local news channel.

Turning to the chess champion, the journalist asked:

'Why d'you play with such wild abandon?'

Nasrudin considered the question for a moment.

'All the other grandmasters start with the opening and work their way to the end game,' he said. 'But as with everything else, I do it the other way round – I start with the end game and work my way back to the opening.'

Water, Ice, Vapour

A frequent traveller, Nasrudin swore he never got sick because he always took water from his own well, and never drank anything but that outside the Land of Fools.

On one occasion, he stuffed a large bottle of the special well water in his check-in luggage, but when he reached his destination in the Land of the Peculiar and the Strange, he found it had acquired a horrid taste.

So, whenever flying out of the Land of Fools, he insisted on taking a supply of the precious liquid in his hand luggage. All was well until, for security reasons, passengers were ordered to place liquids in luggage for the hold.

Clutching a bottle of the well water to his chest, Nasrudin begged to be permitted to take it aboard.

Alas, he was refused.

'The chief of security won't allow it!' spat a guard.

The next time he travelled, the wise fool put the bottle in the freezer overnight. Even though the water was no longer a liquid, it was not allowed on board.

Enraged, Nasrudin worked out a way to pressurize water vapour, and to carry it in a special flask.

Yet again, it was refused by the security guards.

Beside himself with indignation, the wise fool stormed into the office where the security chief was eating his lunch. Slamming a hand down on the wooden desk, he roared:

'This desk is a chair, and that chair is a door!'

The security chief looked up gruffly.

'Who are you and what are you talking about?!' he boomed.

'I am a humble passenger who's eager to learn from you... for you are the one man alive who apparently defies the laws of physics!'

Nonsensical Ageing

While on his travels, Nasrudin journeyed westwards into the Land of Miraculous Mountains, and found it was in a different time zone than the Land of Fools.

Turning his watch back by an hour, he felt reinvigorated.

The way he saw it, he was younger, having shaken off a full hour of time.

Overjoyed, he travelled on westwards, crossing from one time zone to the next.

After many months of travelling, he reached the international date line.

Traversing it by ship, he learned that he had aged a full day all at once – something he regarded as illogical in the extreme.

'I ought to have stayed in the Land of Fools,' he grumbled, 'for at least there, the one place devoted to the nonsensical, you age as you're supposed to.'

Losing One's Head

ne night, Nasrudin dreamt that he had cut off his head with a carving knife and had bled to death before he could raise the alarm.

Waking in a cold sweat, he remembered the dream in all its vivid detail.

Honest by nature, he put on a coat and hurried to the police station.

'I'd like to turn myself in!' he hollered.

'Turn yourself in for what?'

'For cutting off my head in the night.'

The officer looked at Nasrudin in bewilderment.

'You are standing before me with your head on your shoulders,' he countered. 'So, unless I'm missing something, you haven't cut off your head at all.'

Stepping over to a mirror on the wall, Nasrudin saw that his head was indeed still located on his shoulders.

'Hoorah!' he exclaimed jubilantly. 'It's a miracle!'

The duty officer balked at the remark.

'It's more like a dream,' he said.

'No, no, no,' Nasrudin answered. 'I know a dream and I know a miracle – two very different things!'

Pushing his way past the officer, the wise fool hurried to the teahouse, where he held court.

'It was the most extraordinary thing!' he wailed. 'One minute my head had been cut off by my own hand, and the next I was standing in the police station right as rain!'

'Funny,' said the landlord.

'What is?'

'That you were beheaded in the night.'

'What's funny about it?' quipped the wise fool.

'Well,' the teahouse landlord said, 'last night I climbed into your bedroom, slipped into your body, cut off your head, and climbed out again. So, imagine how I felt at seeing you turn up here today with your head back on your shoulders again!'

Urban Camouflage

ord spread through the Land of Fools
that a secret attack force from the Land
of Miraculous Mountains had infiltrated
the kingdom.

Seconded to an elite group of undercover officers,
Captain Nasrudin was ordered to patrol the streets of the
capital. Before taking up his role, he and the others in the
unit were kitted out with special uniforms.

As they were patrolling the city, they were told to
trade their standard desert camouflage in for grey urban
camouflage which would blend in with the buildings.

On the first day of patrol, each one of the elite team was
apprehended by the secret attack force.

Only Captain Nasrudin had evaded capture. Radioing
in to high command, he was ordered to explain the secret
to his stealth.

'Very simple, sir,' he said, over the shortwave radio, 'you see, all the others were dressed in urban camouflage – which made them stick out. I, on the other hand, simply changed back into a T-shirt and jeans, and mingled in with everyone else.'

Relearning

lthough not fond of farming, Nasrudin inherited a smallholding on which there grazed fifty sheep.

He had little affection for the animals, but liked them more than he did dogs – to which he was severely allergic. The thought of using a sheepdog filled him with dread, as he would no doubt be spluttering and itching from morning until night.

So, going against convention, the wise fool taught his cat to herd sheep.

Remarkably, the feline picked up the skill within a day or two. And, elated at not being subjected to canine aggression, the sheep did whatever they were expected to do.

Within a month, all the sheepdogs in the Land of Fools had been replaced by sheepcats. As a result, cats were given new respect, while their canine counterparts were shunned. At the same time, the mouse and rat population thrived, as all the cats in the kingdom were taken up with herding sheep.

One night, Nasrudin had a dream in which his uncle's old sheepdog appeared and begged him to go back to traditional ways.

'But I am allergic to dogs!' the wise fool protested.

The dog growled.

'Your allergy is affecting the entire balance of life!'

'Why don't you dogs simply learn how to catch rats and mice?' asked Nasrudin. 'After all, the cats relearned how to herd sheep.'

The dog growled a second time, more ferociously than before.

'Beware with your advice on relearning!' he snarled. 'Or we may very well relearn to become farmers who live in comfortable houses. That will mean that you farmers and your families will have to go out and live in the dog kennels!'

Waking with a start, Nasrudin hurried out to the kennel, in which his cat was asleep. Stroking it lovingly, he took the animal back inside.

'Your sheepherding days are behind you,' he said.

The Duel

 aving got into a scuffle in the teahouse, Nasrudin was challenged to a duel by a man far younger than himself.

It was arranged that they would meet with pistols the next morning at the edge of the forest.

Arriving at the chosen spot early, the wise fool harangued his huddle of supporters on how he was fearless, and a crack shot. He boasted that he could shoot a blade of grass from a thousand paces, and that he was braver than brave could be.

He was about to lay on the hyperbole even more thickly, when the challenger arrived.

Lean and sure-footed, he was far more impressive than he had seemed in the teahouse the evening before.

Sensing that he was to be unmasked as a coward and as the worst shot in the kingdom – or even worse, that his life was about to be snuffed out – Nasrudin thought fast.

As soon as the challenger was near, he waved the duelling pistols away.

'Didn't I tell you that I never duel with pistols?' he exclaimed.

'Swords?' the young man shot back. 'Shall we duel with swords?'

The wise fool huffed and puffed at the very thought.

'So old-fashioned!' he barked.

'Then what *is* your chosen weapon?'

Nasrudin reached down and plucked two identical blades of grass.

'These,' he said.

The challenger scoffed.

'How foolish do you think me to be?' he gasped. 'To fight like children with pathetic blades of grass, when we could be inflicting real damage on one another with duelling pistols or swords!'

The wise fool regarded the youth sideways on.

'On the contrary,' he riposted. 'Leaving this place without injury and with our honour intact sounds like anything but foolishness to me!'

The Shortest Book

ince childhood, Nasrudin had wanted to publish a book, and had worked at the manuscript for years.

Everyone in the teahouse knew that the wise fool regarded himself as the greatest novelist in the history of the Land of Fools – or rather the greatest novelist who had never published anything at all.

Unable to stand the mockery any longer, he took his manuscript to a publisher and asked whether they would consider it. To his surprise the editor agreed, with one caveat.

'The price of ink has gone up,' he was informed, 'and so we'll have to cut it down a little.'

Nasrudin weighed the manuscript in his hand.

'It's a thousand pages,' he answered, 'and so I daresay you can make a nip and a tuck.'

The editor smiled.

'Once we've edited it, we will be in touch,' he said.

A month later, the revision was ready. To Nasrudin's horror, the thousand pages had been whittled down to no more than a hundred.

'It'll be a short, punchy novel,' the editor said. 'If the price of ink doesn't go up, we'll release it next month.'

But the price of ink *did* go up.

Accordingly, a second edit was done – reducing the manuscript from a hundred pages to thirty.

Then, the price of ink went up yet again.

And again.

Eventually, Nasrudin was called in for an editorial meeting and shown the manuscript.

Rather, he was shown a single page…

…on which there was a single word.

Or rather, a single capital letter:

I

Nasrudin flinched.

'You have reduced a thousand pages of wonder to a single letter,' he hissed.

Glancing across the desk at the would-be author, the editor-in-chief raised an eyebrow.

'A single letter it may be,' he said, 'but we've spared no expense in representing it with the panache it deserves.'

Crestfallen, the wise fool tapped a fingertip to the solitary letter.

'Can't you give it another letter, you know – to keep it company? Or at least print my name as well?'

The editor winced.

'Can't afford the ink,' he said.

'But I had dreams of being known as the author of the longest book in the kingdom's history.'

Again, the editor squirmed in his chair.

'Why don't you write a sequel?' he offered.

Nasrudin's face lit up.

'*Yes!*' he gasped. 'That's what I'll do. It'll be a great big sequel.'

The editor grinned.

'We could call it "*U*",' he said.

Speaking With Certainty

Nasrudin was asked by a Foolslander how one could tell the age of a person with certainty.

'Well,' he answered knowingly, 'it's remarkably simple. You know, don't you, that trees have rings for every year they have been alive?'

'Yes,' said the fool, 'to work out a tree's age, you just count the rings.'

The wise fool dipped his head in a nod.

'Well, to know the age of a person you simply take a saw, chop them in two around the waist, and count the rings.'

'But humans don't have rings like trees!' exclaimed the fool.

'Have you ever sawn a person in half and inspected them?'

'No,' lisped the fool.

'Well, how can you speak with such certainty, then?' retorted Nasrudin.

Soul Flame

asrudin had a dream in which a candle was burning beside his bed.

When the candle's flame went out, he himself dropped dead.

On waking, the wise fool found that there was indeed a lit candle next to the bed in which he had been sleeping. Believing the dream had come true, he assumed the candle bore a soul flame that was somehow tethered to his own mortality.

Having explained the dream and the significance of the candle to his wife, Nasrudin said he would never allow the soul flame to go out.

The most rational person alive, his wife told him to stop being so stupid.

Anxious that she would blow the candle out when he went into town, Nasrudin took it with him. Despite there being a breeze, he managed to protect the flame, and reached the teahouse with it burning as brightly as it had done in the dream.

It wasn't long before one of the fools asked why Nasrudin would have a lit candle with him on such a clear summer's day.

The wise fool explained the details of the dream.

'The soul flame is somehow connected to my life,' he said. 'If it were to be extinguished, I would drop dead.'

Word of the curious link between the flame and its owner spread.

Within a day or two, fools everywhere had begun believing that, were their candles to go out, then they themselves would drop dead.

Within a week, the tradition of keeping a soul flame lit in order to protect one's own life had spread to the neighbouring kingdoms as well.

Within a month, everyone in the known world believed it – everyone, that is, except for Nasrudin's wife.

One morning, while her husband was dressing, she snuffed out the soul flame.

'There!' she shouted. 'The flame's out and you're not dead!'

Wailing, the wise fool clutched both hands to his heart.

'I may not be dead in the waking world,' he scowled, 'but how d'you know of my condition in the landscape of my dreams?!'

Splinter of a Star

ne night on his way home from the teahouse, Nasrudin spotted something shining on the ground.

Curious as to what it could be, he went over and picked it up.

The object was a simple shard of broken glass.

Holding it to the light of the moon, the wise fool assumed it was a piece of star that had somehow splintered off a celestial body and fallen to earth.

Next morning, taking the piece of star to the palace, Nasrudin demanded an audience with the king.

It being the Land of Fools, and the monarch being as dim-witted as everyone else, the wise fool was admitted, along with his shard of broken glass.

Once in the throne room, he was asked to explain himself.

'Your Majesty,' Nasrudin intoned obsequiously, 'the Land of Fools has been blessed with a magnificent fragment of the heavens!'

Craning forwards, the king regarded the piece of broken glass.

'Where is it from?' he asked in awe.

'From a distant galaxy!'

The monarch thought for a moment, the tip of a royal index finger tapping the end of the royal chin.

Nasrudin cleared his throat.

'I would surmise that it splintered off the wisest star in all the universe,' he mused, 'and travelled through an eternity of time and space to grace us here in the Land of Fools.'

'Grace us with what purpose?' asked the king.

Bowing deeply, the wise fool stepped forwards to the throne.

The precious fragment of a star cupped in his hands, he offered it to his monarch.

'The purpose,' he whispered, 'could only be to pledge homage to the wisest sovereign who ever lived.'

With thumb and forefinger, the king picked the shard of broken glass and held it close to his face.

'This is the Land of Fools,' he said, 'and I am its foolish king...'

'And what a sublime foolish king and ruler of fools you are!' Nasrudin broke in unctuously.

'I am a foolish king who was taught to read,' the monarch went on.

Maintaining his composure, the wise fool wondered what the king was getting at.

'A foolish king who was taught to read,' the king repeated, 'and who knows enough to comprehend there is no tomato sauce on the distant star from which this little fragment of glass ketchup bottle fell!'

Out of Sight, Out of Mind

he king of the Land of Fools taxed his people extra heavily, so as to raise funds to build himself a colossal palace.

As opulent as it was vulgar, the structure was an eyesore that could not be ignored.

Like everyone else, Nasrudin couldn't help but see it. For, almost every window in the entire kingdom had a view upon it. Even when toiling in his field, the wise fool could not help but see the palace he so loathed.

Born into a lowly farming family, Nasrudin was never expected to be anything other than a poor farmer.

But a few weeks after the palace had been completed, he was consumed with burning ambition.

While all the other fools in the kingdom lay about like Lotus Eaters, the wise fool began wheeling and dealing, and doing what he could to scale the social ladder at double speed.

In the teahouse one evening, his best friend enquired why Nasrudin drove himself so hard.

'It's because I hate that palace more than anything in the world!' he exclaimed.

His friend shrugged.

'What has the palace got to do with the crazed way you push yourself?'

Nasrudin took a sip of his tea.

'I plan to become the king's vizier,' he answered. 'I have it all mapped out.'

The best friend grimaced.

'But if you were to secure that position you'd be expected to live in the very palace you hate.'

Nasrudin smiled from the corner of his mouth.

'Exactly,' he said. 'The one place in the entire kingdom where I shall not be able to see the damned palace of the king!'

The Monkey's Hand

In art school, Nasrudin had learned about the portrait painter who represented a duchess's hand as the paw of a monkey.

Through the ruse, the aristocrat depicted was so alarmed at the blunder that she neglected to notice any of the lesser shortcomings.

Having enjoyed a glittering career as a portrait painter, the wise fool was invited to capture the likeness of the queen of the Land of Fools. A woman of indescribable pomposity and avarice, Her Majesty was the very last person Nasrudin wanted to paint.

Cajoled by the royal vizier, he realized he could not refuse.

Once the queen had sat for a few minutes, Nasrudin bowed deeply and pledged to deliver the finished portrait the following week.

Through days and nights, the palace buzzed with anticipation.

Never one to miss a chance for self-aggrandizement, the queen invited a who's who of dignitaries to witness the unveiling in the throne room.

Bugles resounded, and the high and mighty of the Land of Fools gathered around an easel shrouded in miles of black silk.

The queen nodded to the artist. He in turn jerked away the cloth.

A communal gasp echoed around the throne room.

Rather than paint the paw of a monkey on the body of a lady, Nasrudin had painted the hand of a lady on the body of a monkey.

Royal guards leapt forward and seized the artist.

Before they dragged him away, the wise fool was given a chance to explain himself.

'I do apologize,' said Nasrudin. 'Give me a little time, and I will correct the error of my ways.'

Fuming with rage, the queen demanded to know how much time was required.

The wise fool thought for a moment.

'No more than a minute or two,' he said curtly. 'After all, it's just a single paw that needs to be modified.'

Leap Tradition

In a bid to keep up with neighbouring kingdoms, the Land of Fools decreed that a host of new cultural practices would be written into the statute books as ancient traditions.

With no other fools available, Nasrudin was made Secretary of Ancient Traditions – the administrator charged with deciding which day would be reserved for which tradition.

Adept at nonsensical bureaucracy, the wise fool excelled in the role. Within a day and a half, he had amassed three hundred and sixty-five traditions – one for every day of the year.

A panel of fools listened to the recommendations, then congratulated the Secretary of Ancient Traditions. The meeting was about to be adjourned when a low-level official raised a hand.

'What about leap years?' he asked.

'What about them?' enquired the wise fool.

'Well, on February 29th what will be the tradition we celebrate?'

Widening his eyes, Nasrudin thought for a moment.

'February 29th will be the day devoted to the ancient tradition of celebrating traditions,' he said.

Numerical Rearrangement

asrudin's bank statement arrived, sending him into a state of panic.

The month before, he had had a thousand dinars in his account, and now he apparently only had one dinar left.

Whimpering, he hurried to the bank.

After much pleading he was admitted into the office of the manager.

'Last month I had a thousand dinars,' he said, 'and now I have only one.'

The manager looked up from his papers.

'It seems as though you've been lax with your spending,' he said.

'There must be a mistake,' stammered Nasrudin.

His face flushed with ire, the bank manager regarded the customer with loathing.

'Numbers never lie!' he spat.

'Perhaps they're not lying,' corrected the wise fool. 'But rather, they've been playing hide-and-seek with one another. Perhaps we could coax the *one* to go back into the thousands column, and encourage all the naughty little *zeros* to come out, come out, wherever they are?!'

Blisters and Pearls

While plodding into town, Nasrudin felt a little piece of grit in his shoe.

Even though it caused him discomfort, he left it where it was.

By the time he reached town, his foot was blistered and bleeding.

A friend in the teahouse asked what was going on.

'I've got a little piece of grit in my shoe,' Nasrudin explained.

'Well, why don't you take it out instead of hobbling around as you are?'

'Because,' answered the wise fool gruffly, 'I'm leaving it in there in the hope it turns into a pearl on the way home!'

Blue Sunsets

Nasrudin developed a phobia of the colour yellow.

For a long while he kept it to himself, until the deep-seated fear began getting in the way of ordinary life. Whenever he glimpsed the sun in the sky, he would wail with terror. And whenever he spotted an amber traffic light, he'd get out of his car and run for the hills.

At his wits' end, the wise fool sought out the most celebrated psychologist in the Land of Fools.

Once the doctor had heard the condition described, and had scribbled a page of notes, he held up a photograph of a bright-yellow canary.

Leaping to his feet, Nasrudin ran round and round.

When the patient was calmer, the psychologist showed him a second card, bearing a picture of a lemon.

Again, the patient leapt up and ran about, even more disturbed than before.

The doctor scribbled another page of notes, before turning to the patient.

'When did you start feeling so fearful at seeing yellow?' he asked.

Nasrudin pondered the question.

'Since the day sunsets turned blue,' he said.

Life Swap

ore broke than he had ever been in his life, Nasrudin had resorted to living on the streets and picking through litter bins for scraps.

While in this wretched state, he had an idea that had the possibility of flipping his fortunes around. Walking over to the royal palace, the building he loathed with all his heart, he requested an audience with the king.

'I have a question to ask His Majesty,' said the wise fool. 'I promise it will take no more than a minute.'

'If it does, you'll be taken to the dungeons,' barked the guard, opening the gate.

The wise fool was led into the throne room, where the king was sitting on his throne. Awed by the contrast with his own life, he took in the great platters of sweetmeats, the lavish furnishings, the throne, and the royal crown perched squarely on the royal head.

'I understand you have a question to ask me?' the monarch growled imperiously.

'Yes, Your Majesty.'

'And I understand you have promised that this audience will take no more than a minute, otherwise you will be dragged to the dungeons?'

'Yes, Your Majesty.'

'Well, I'd say you have about ten seconds left before the guards come and take you away – so I suggest you spit out your question double speed.'

Standing as tall as he could manage in his filthy rags, Nasrudin held out both hands, palms upturned.

'In the name of God, will you please swap your life with mine?!'

The king clapped his hands.

'Throw this man out!'

As he dragged the wise fool back to the street, the guard asked incredulously what had been going through his head.

For a fraction of a moment, there was a glint in the beggar's eye.

'Imagine if the king had said YES!' whispered Nasrudin.

Finis

THE MISADVENTURES OF
THE MYSTIFYING NASRUDIN

TAHIR SHAH

THE PEREGRINATIONS OF
THE PERPLEXING NASRUDIN

TAHIR SHAH

THE VOYAGES AND
VICISSITUDES OF NASRUDIN

TAHIR SHAH

TRAVELS WITH NASRUDIN

TAHIR SHAH

A REQUEST

If you enjoyed this book, please review it on your favourite online retailer or review website.

Reviews are an author's best friend.

To stay in touch with Tahir Shah, and to hear about his upcoming releases before anyone else, please sign up for his mailing list:

 http://tahirshah.com/newsletter

And to follow him on social media, please go to any of the following links:

http://www.twitter.com/humanstew

@tahirshah999

http://www.facebook.com/TahirShahAuthor

http://www.youtube.com/user/tahirshah999

http://www.pinterest.com/tahirshah

https://www.goodreads.com/tahirshahauthor

http://www.tahirshah.com